A HOLE IN
THE WIND

Praise for A Hole In The Wind

"Horner invites the reader into the wounds of loneliness with sensitivity born of experiencing human nature at its best and worst moments. Not since Arthur Miller has a writer come to literary art with more agony and a barometer for the human condition."

> —Gerald L. Gamache, therapist for survivors of the Chernobyl nuclear disaster; diplomate, American Association of Psychological Specialties; diplomate, American Psychotherapeutic Association.

"Carl S. Horner's *A Hole in the Wind* takes the reader right out there with the guys on the bikes, guys trying to win races but who come to find a greater victory, a sudden maturity during tragic crisis. This novel has a compelling, artistic passion that raises its authentic excitement into a moral understanding, a fresh hope of how the world might be."

> —Andrew Dillon, author of poetry and of literary explication published in *Worcester Review, Connecticut Review, Kansas Quarterly, Arizona Quarterly*, and other journals.

"...deceptively straightforward... Horner's story captures the heart-break of alienation and the heart-pounding excitement of racing competition, and his prose pulls a reader into a world in which the smallest detail, a wind draft or a poorly designed drainage grate, can make the difference between victory or defeat, life or death."

> —Larry Baker, author of *The Flamingo Rising*, a novel and Hallmark Hall of Fame Presentation.

"*A Hole in the Wind* inspires people to channel their interests into things worth doing, a message long overdue in American media."
　　—James Caputo, high school teacher and alcohol abuse counselor.

"... taut, fast-paced... this is... a literary victory on par with Lance Armstrong's Tour de France triumph."
　　—Scott C. Benyacko, middle school English teacher and author of *Remembering Jenny*.

"A brilliant psychological dichotomy of bullying as an act of cowardice. Carl S. Horner has nailed this social plight right on the head!"
　　—GA Watkins, author of *Rocklandheart, a novel*.

"Horner simultaneously examines the virtues of sport and the brutal human consequences of the desire for supremacy. With sharp dialogue and fresh language, he presents a Holden Caulfield who seeks not to escape but to engage the injustices of the world on honest terms. Meanwhile, he evokes the physical thrill of bicycle racing and illuminates the complexities of that sport without condescending to the uninformed."
　　—Michael Matejka, author of *Poor, Blind, and Naked*.

"This novel passes the 2:00 AM test: I had to force myself to put it down and go to sleep."
　　—Annemarie Halback, aspiring author.

A HOLE
IN THE WIND

CARL S. HORNER

A WD Book
Los Angeles • California

WD Books is an imprint of
WD Publishers, a division of GES Communications Inc.
1127 S. King Street • San Gabriel, CA 91776

WD Books, its logo and WD Publishers are trademarks of
GES Communications Inc.
http://www.wdpublishers.com

Library of Congress Cataloging-in-Publication Data

Horner, Carl S., 1945-
  A hole in the wind / Carl S. Horner.-- 1st WD books ed.
     p. cm.
  ISBN 0-9723593-1-1 (alk. paper)
1. Teenage boys--Fiction. 2. Jacksonville (Fla.)--Fiction.
3. Bicycle racing--Fiction. I. Title.

PS3608.O7628H65 2005
813'.6--dc22

                                        2005003870

Book design by Aden-A-Wat Creations
Manufactured in the United States of America.

For Helane,
my first riding buddy
and eternal wife and friend

Acknowledgments

Endless memories of Bart Weiss, David Buell, David Jacobs, David Berk, Kent Jones, Sam Myrick, Mary Alice Myers, Stacy Freedman, and Beal McIlvain, the founders of Tamarack Racing Team, compelled me to evoke the fictive life of Colby Fowler in *A Hole in the Wind*.

Special, special thanks to Page Edwards, Holly Horner, Darien Andreu, Matt Holmquist, Frank Upchurch, Barbara Sloan, Bill Hannon, Steve Watson, Bill Lanni, Rob Brown, Amanda Vargo, and Todd Neville for editing drafts of the novel; to Helen Turner, Ron and Jan McVey, Brian Wilson, Kacee Lingner, Fran Schar, Rufus McClure, W. D. Snodgrass, David Kirby, David Poyer, Robert Olen Butler, and GA and Deni Watkins for caring about and enlarging my passion and for believing in *A Hole in the Wind*; and to Nancy Pelletier, Joe Provenza, Tracey Cotto, and Terry Bennett for copying and for mailing manuscripts.

ONE

Of course, the two psychos had to go for each other's throats the whole time it took them to pack their camping gear into the school van. Coach already told these boys to hurry up and get their stuff loaded, get ready to ride their bikes to Gold Head State Park to practice racing for the weekend. But they kept bludgeoning each other with insults, honking themselves into a y-chromosome spasm.

It's the most selfish thing, Colby Fowler thought. When he hitched up with the bike team in September, he had tried to talk to these put-down junkies on training rides. Put-down junkies—these two piranhas ate dinner together, stayed at each other's houses for the night. They hated each other's guts, but they were best friends, all right. They called each other best friends. They called Fowler that new freak from Pittsburgh.

During his first week at Coleman Academy in Jacksonville, Florida, he had tried to share his bike magazines with them in class and had even invited them to eat lunch with him one day. But there was always something forbidden, something stingy about their words, and they only loosened up when they got free of him.

Fowler only had a year of club racing in his legs when his tenth-grade English teacher talked him into riding for Coleman. He liked and trusted his new teacher and coach. He liked how the man pushed him, how he didn't think of him as a rookie when he'd jump and make him chase him, how he knew he wanted to attack—do all the things the other boys did.

But he felt unconnected. This wasn't just testing the new kid on the chopping block. This wasn't hazing. Five weeks of riding two, four, sometimes five or six hours together out on the road, and the two other boys still made him feel like they were towing around a U-Haul trailer. They didn't say anything. They didn't have to.

Feeling them orbiting around him now in the stupor of their private wars, uncertainty gnawing at the inner walls of his confidence—defining odd moments in his expression when fear and courage struggled through his eyes at the same time, he wandered over to Coach Wood Kelly.

He looked old for his age. Already six feet, four inches, he was the tallest boy in his class, and he had a few gray hairs sneaking out of a cowlick on the back of his head.

"You need anything?" Kelly asked, when Fowler offered to hold his bike.

Fowler shook his head, but couldn't talk.

Tapping at his Mickey Mouse watch, Kelly stepped between the two other boys. "How about you, Burkhart? You and this other magpie of yours over here. You guys ready to hurt?"

Burkhart stiffened his lips, his face pale, tense—cold, like the blue stones in his eyes. "The question is, old man, are y-ou ready to hurt?"

Kelly suppressed a smile and knocked on

Burkhart's helmet. "Listen up, guys. Take it easy till we get to Old Mandarin Road. Then, go ahead and open the cage."

TWO

Traffic was light for a Friday afternoon on San Jose Boulevard, east of the new restaurants, shopping centers, and bold, sprawling office buildings creeping toward Old Mandarin. Even the Bubba trucks with their enameled gun racks squatted to catch their breath in shaded spots along the St. Johns River, quivering green and silver in the white October sunlight.

Up came Roberto Ruiz, turning a poker face on Burkhart. When he didn't meet the team at Coleman as planned, Kelly had worried that his work had black-holed him in his office for the weekend.

Fowler liked Roberto. He liked how the guy put his grip on everything he did, like a matador riveting his fingers into his cape. He liked how he gripped his bike.

He studied Darwin's pick for the fastest sprint in

Jacksonville—the way he shot Gatorade into the corner of his mouth, the way he held his bottle, the way he could drink and spin his crank plate at the same time, not losing form, not dropping his cadence. Fowler locked his eyes onto the way he put his bottle back into its cage, as if he hadn't moved his arm—as if by magic.

The five riders pulled off San Jose Boulevard and stroked easy miles down Beauclerc Road and on down Scott Mill Access, spinning past new two-story brick and cedar homes and older estates obscuring their peek-a-boo opulence behind octopus trees and long stone walls with iron gates.

No one said a word. Not for two miles.

Fowler looked over at Roberto's finish-line eyes, wedged into the silence. Adrenalin twitched in his arms, in his legs. He felt jumpy in the stomach, like he was getting ready to swallow blood.

Kelly shoved at his back and signaled to Burkhart to take the front of the paceline at the turn onto Old Mandarin Road. "Push yourselves hard now!" he shouted, his voice cracking like a starting pistol. "And push each other!"

Fowler clicked a bigger gear. The air thickened in his lungs. He inched closer to Burkhart, feeling his bike lighten in the draft of his rear wheel. He dropped his head—he ramped another gear—and kept hammering his legs into his pedals.

Burkhart pulled the other riders a gutsy three quarters of a mile, then disappeared, leaving Fowler alone at the front to drill his bike into the wind.

Fowler tried to hold onto Burkhart's pace—he even tried to push it—but his legs were already burning.

He cranked out of his saddle, but Roberto motored past him.

He stayed up, cranking harder to catch Burkhart's wheel at the rear of the train, but his legs felt heavy—and springy like rubber bands.

He felt dizzy.

The asphalt started boiling in front of him.

He wobbled his bike a few seconds into the dirt beside the road.

His handlebars bounced—jarring his grip—he

thought he was going down—but his wheels caught solid ground.

He felt his heart beating in his ears—beating in his throat.

He lost peripheral vision. He might have blacked out—but he heard Coach Kelly whistling beside him. Kelly had dropped back when he saw Fowler in trouble. He whistled a second time and then pulled him back up to the other riders.

Roberto had talked Burkhart and Billy Huffman into cutting the pace, but Burkhart was glaring at the black numbers on his Cateye computer. He was glaring at Fowler.

Everyone spun the stiffness out of their legs for a quarter of a mile along the narrow road, darkened by thick canopy oaks. The wind chattered like a worried spirit through the leaves above their heads. They tunneled another half mile into the swishing woods until the underpass widened, the pavement brightened, and spilled out over fields of maturing orange trees. Orange fruit hung like swollen Christmas tree lights.

Fifty meters into the clearing, Burkhart rocked his bike into a sprint—striking for the center of the road. "Oranges!" he blared like someone jumping away from a fire. "Come on! I smell oranges! O-ranges!" he shouted a second and third time—digging into his pedals—digging into the wind.

Ruiz and Kelly snapped themselves onto his draft, their industry hot and unyielding, towing Fowler and Huffman in their fury.

"You might as well have thrown us a rope," Roberto growled at Burkhart's back.

Dodging right, dodging left, Burkhart tried to fight himself off the front, but Ruiz and Kelly kept blocking him, feeding him into the wind. He tried to break out ahead of them—break them off his wheel. But he couldn't find his legs. He couldn't find his eyes. He stumbled off his line.

Ruiz and Kelly burst out of their saddles—splitting the three boys apart like they had tilted the road.

THREE

The sun started rolling itself down for the night by six-fifteen, spilling its slow blood light into the trees and the finger lakes at Gold Head State Park.

Fowler bent into the darkness flooding the ground at his feet. He thought about heading off by himself, deep into the kindred mist of the woods, but he pulled his wind jacket out of his sleeping bag and looked up at the two cold stones in Burkhart's eyes.

The campsite wasn't close enough to the water, according to Burkhart. The fire wasn't big enough. The fire wasn't hot enough. Kelly wasn't cooking anything safe to eat, and Kelly didn't have anything planned for the rest of the evening, nothing worthy of Burkhart's time.

"You turn everything we do into a slug-fest,"

Fowler said. He stiffened with his words—braiding, hurting his fingers.

Burkhart shook a banana at Fowler but didn't bother to look at him. "Hey, don't y-ou even talk to me," he said and sank into the grass beside Kelly. "Everybody's in my face all the time about what I should and shouldn't do."

"You've only been doing that to us for the last five weeks," Fowler said.

"People ought to live like cats. I'm telling you something. I ain't no pack animal."

"You act like an animal."

"That's because I'd rather b-e an animal—a raccoon would be nice. No, a rain forest lizard—no, a cat." Burkhart leaned forward and pinched a snail shell out of the dirt he was kicking with the heel of his shoe. "I'll tell you something here for sure. I'm going to take my own space."

He glowered at everybody. "Cats, cats, live like c-ats." He snapped his teeth shut. He rolled his eyes in the dark glow of the campfire.

In his mind, Fowler drifted back to Pittsburgh,

to a night when one of his cats kept wailing to get in, wailing to get out, wailing to get back in, wailing to get back out.

It was the most selfish thing. Fowler couldn't do his homework. He started to get up, to push back his chair, but his border collie jumped off his bed, stiff-legged himself into the living room. Whatever happened next, Fowler could only guess, but he heard a lot of spitting and bodies crashing into walls and a drop-leaf table.

Typical Burkhart, he thought. And the worst part, he knew this psycho had roped him into playing this game—suckered him into doing the opposite of what his burning insides were telling him to do—now to the point of no return, now that he wasn't backing down.

"I hate to ring your bell," Fowler said. "But you forgot something—you forgot to tell us where you cats like to stick your noses."

Burkhart glared at Fowler across the brightening firelight. He bladed his middle finger out of a fist he'd been pressing into his hand. "In case you haven't figured it out yet, Colby c-at. No one likes you here," he said. "This freak—see, right there it is. This freak doesn't click on his messages like a normal human being, besides the fact you're not n-ormal."

"Why don't you do us all a favor, Burkhart, and camp somewhere out in the middle of that lake," Harrison Blount spoke up. He unfolded his enormous arms from his chest. "You can feel sorry for yourself out there under that moon all night, you little narcissist."

Kelly had cajoled Blount into driving the van and camping with the team for the weekend. Because Kelly's teacher friend looked so threatening—with cutting black eyes and a furious red and gray beard—students treated him with caution, with the fear they were stepping into the bad company of a grizzly bear.

Fowler studied Blount's shoulders and the complex muscles and veins that ran like fire hoses through his arms. He pictured the man who came out one summer to break up the patio behind his house in Pittsburgh. How he had swung his twenty-pound sledge like it were made of Styrofoam.

Billy Huffman butted in—started to ask a question—but hesitated, sounding like he was squeezing Vaseline between his tongue and the roof of his mouth.

With his huge, dark eyes and narrow face, Huffman looked like a beagle puppy. The football players had nicknamed him "Beagle Boy," but he swore he'd beat up anybody else who called him that, including Burkhart, including even Kelly.

"So, Mr. Blount." He tried to speak again, his confidence loosening as his eyes ricocheted off Burkhart. "So let's shoot him."

It was no kidding. Blount had a gun—more like the cut-down version of a Civil War cannon the size of a wheel chair. First week of class, Burkhart was snoring his brains out like he always did, and Blount got fed up with it. Shushing at everybody not to squeal, not to giggle, not to blow his coup, he exploded that rude awakening right beside Burkhart's desk. The room shifted like ball bearings.

Got Burkhart's attention, all right. He came off the floor, desk and all, kicking his feet into the air.

Chortling to himself, Fowler looked across the campfire at Huffman, crawling on his hands and knees toward a bag of bike-cleaning rags. But he stopped, working his fingers under the grass and into the dirt. He shook his head and clicked his teeth. "Happiest day of my life."

"Yeah, well at least I don't snore like a school bus every time I sleep in class."

"So give it up, Burkhart. You got busted. And don't you think I'm ever letting you forget it either. Because I'm not."

Teacher stories got Fowler thinking. Back in Pittsburgh, back when getting out of bed in the morning didn't mean another death sentence, he had this science teacher. Boo-Boo Neanderthal Man would get a grip on this bar across the top of his chalkboard and hang up there every time someone couldn't answer one of his looney questions.

They could make the poor clinger hang like that sometimes five minutes before he started screaming names. But that's when they had to get careful, though, because he'd start knocking points off everybody's quarter average if some nerd kid couldn't dig some clever word or figure out of a notebook. But he kept hanging up there till he got his answer.

Fowler could see Boo-Boo's uncombed brown hair storming all over the back of his head. Not Einstein—more like a monkey stuffed into a white lab coat.

Feeling his hands warming his face, he stretched out his long legs. He looked over at Burkhart cracking sticks into halves and quarters in the dithering firelight.

"I'm trying to mind my own b-usiness." Burkhart stared at the ground and broke another stick in half. "Coach here has to go and poke me in the neck about some freak who lifts whole ox carts by himself and then starts running through the sewers with some other weenie bleeding all over his back. Like I don't have better things to do than memorize English ninety-two hours a day. Hey, next thing I know, he's making us all go outside. He's yelling—hey, he's yelling about how we need some t-angible experience, whatever that means."

Dropping his eyes now to half mast, Burkhart scowled at Kelly. "Forty-five—no, forty-seven and a half minutes, he makes us hump each other up and down that campus. Not piggy-back. N-ot the easy way. He had a better plan. Strapped over our shoulders. And the whole time he's back up there yelling we've got it better than that freak in the sewers. I don't know, it was raining, and I had to carry Huffman. The walrus had to go and rip a hundred and ninety-three scrambled egg f-arts before I got him down that big hill by the river."

Huffman threatened to stand up. He slapped the ground beside him. "So I didn't hear you begging for no second ride."

"Hey, like any n-ormal person, I dropped the hooting pig, but n-oooo—Coach makes me start all over again, screaming about those freaking sewers and how I have to keep his head up, or he'll d-rown."

Kelly nudged Roberto on the arm. "Well, did you finish the book after that?"

"What c-hoice did you give me? Finish it or carry Huffman to C-incinnati and back, he says. I'm telling you. That's the first book I've ever read in my life. The thing's got five thousand pages, too."

"Did you have any weirdo teachers in Columbia, Ro?"

"In Columbia, things were different." Roberto hesitated, smiling at Kelly with greater sympathy. "It was a matter of honor—you were the lucky one who got the chance to go to school."

"I had a lunatic teacher in junior high," Kelly said. "If he caught you talking or passing notes or chewing gum, he'd reach into a jar of formaldehyde he kept on his desk, and he'd throw a huge cow eye at you."

"I'm not even going to listen to this one," Burkhart said.

"Yep, history teacher. If you caught the eye, you only had to carry it back to his desk. But if you ducked, or if you dropped the slimy thing, then he made you hold both poles of an electric generator he had on permanent loan from the science lab. That was one hair-raising class, let me tell you. One girl named Buffie—now, she had a mean right arm, like every boy in class found out the hard way. He eyeballed her for sleeping. Maybe so, but she pulled that thing out of the air and threw it back sixteen times as hard."

Huffman cackled, turning a pine cone over in his hands. "She threw it at the teacher?"

"Great pitch. Hit old what's-his-name right in the middle of his forty-eight inch stomach. We all insisted a deal's a deal, so Buffie got to turn the crank while that la-la farmer held the generator poles and his hair flew up. We loved him, and we loved that class. Learned our stuff, too, guys."

"So Coach," Huffman said. "He ever throw that thing at you?"

"One day, I was whispering to the kid behind me—something, I think, about the monkey bars in gym class. I look up and here comes that eyeball, shaking and spitting big drops of formaldehyde all over the morons on the front row."

"Did you catch it?" Huffman screeched.

"How well do you know me?"

"He dropped it!" Huffman and Burkhart roared at the same time.

"Ok, you nuts, you mosquitoes," Kelly said. He stood up and tugged at Fowler's yellow wind jacket. "Do whatever you want till eleven, so long as it's legal, honest, and non-disgusting. Everybody ready at nine tomorrow for the hundred big ones."

"Hey, too bad Blount can't ride with us." Burkhart jerked a few gray hairs out of Blount's chaotic beard. "But Campy and Shimano haven't come up with brakes that fit bear claws. And anyway, old grizzly brains here would crush the bike."

"Time someone ties the knot in this kid's filthy lips, Kelly," Blount said.

"Sounds good to me. Want some help?"

"I think I can carry the little orifice to the baptism."

Blount folded Burkhart across his shoulder and

started walking toward a boat ramp that yawned out over the lake.

"Hey, Hairy Harry, go play with your mother back there in the woods." Burkhart squirmed and searched for Blount's belt. "I'm suing you for student abuse, I hope you know. Hey, I'm telling you. I'm allergic to something in your fur. Seriously, you've got to put me down now, or I might have to hurt you."

He flailed his arms and legs into Blount's chest and the back of his leg. He flailed the air. But Blount just kept tightening his grip like a vise and walked on down the wooden ramp.

"Come on! It's cold out here tonight, you freaking p-elt! You're going to make me si—"

Grabbing Burkhart's foot and wrist, the man-beast flung him into the night. Sprawling, screaming, kicking—laughing—Burkhart disappeared beneath a burst of silver water in the lake.

FOUR

After assuring Burkhart that his so-called organic buckwheat pancakes, with water-chilled apple slices and almond syrup, were not quite the worst breakfast he had ever eaten in his life, Kelly cranked off early Sunday morning by himself. He had asked Roberto to loosen up with him a bit on the roller-coaster roads outside the park before the final training ride back to Jacksonville, but Roberto had always dreamed of living in the woods by a lake and wanted to spend his last hours holding onto Eden. The three boys were walking in the woods with Blount.

A western artery snaked its way deeper and deeper into land too forgotten, too coarse for a road. The rough pavement looked more like an abandoned driveway than a tertiary road, mining its way to nowhere. The only signs even of crude engineering were an unsteady wooden bridge over a tight-running creek and a quarter mile of broken fence lines crouching a few meters in the dark forest. The low morning sun wedged its spots of golden light through the trees that stretched like a lid over the steaming road.

Rifle and occasional shotgun rounds split the silence in the distance ahead of him. Kelly had read and had seen documentaries about children caught by stray gunfire. In the rush of their excitement, hunters might hallucinate, might see an animal instead of a person. One sober middle-aged businessman had mistaken a lady for a deer. She was hanging laundry in her own backyard.

But Kelly was wearing a white and florescent orange cycling jersey—colors more brilliant than a hunter's orange vest, he reassured himself. And deer season didn't open till November.

A violent bend in the road led him between two rolling fields of weeds and wild grass. Four scruffy-looking men in beige, green, and brown camouflage shirts and pants stood on the pavement three hundred meters ahead. They were shooting into the trees north of the clearing.

One man caught sight of Kelly's bright jersey coming toward them and elbowed the man next to him. What they said Kelly could only imagine, but the word spread, and the four men shuffled themselves into a barricade, crossing their guns in front of them. Three more men climbed out of the field to the north, and stood staring, first at Kelly and then at their friends, spread like thick rhinos across the road.

Turn around! Turn around! Voices nagged inside Kelly's head. He could see the faces in front of him now, wrinkling into mocking grins.

He aimed his bike at the center of the wall of men. Someone stepped back of the line just before he hit them, and Kelly shot through the hole in the barricade.

One man with crimson splotches on his face shouted at him—he jeered and shouted something about cutting him open.

But the friction ended with that. Kelly heard

gunfire storming back into the trees behind him—he
heard the men firing again at their imaginary
victims in the woods.

FIVE

The road twisted, labored its way through thickets and brief clearings for another eight miles before Kelly found himself gazing into a four-lane highway. Cars and eighteen-wheel rigs clamored past him—rattling at violent speeds—seventy, eighty miles per hour. With no map—with no knowledge of how far he'd have to ride before he discovered a new and safer route back to the park—with the memory of so many bike riders slaughtered like raccoons and armadillos on highways just like this one, he turned in the direction of the dark trees and tunneled back into the forest.

Granny-gear the hills, he thought. Take lots of breaks—they'll go home for lunch.

Two of the men were loading beer coolers and hunting gear into their trucks when Kelly rolled into their sight. One whistled—he swallowed two fingers into his mouth and fired a signal to the five other gunmen, scrambling like wolves out of the northern field.

Turn around! the voices shrieked.

Kelly clicked a bigger gear.

Someone whistled again, and all seven dark figures poured across the road like a river of evil thoughts.

One man raised his rifle. Then another beside him—the man with the crimson splotches on his cheeks.

Kelly flew straight at them. He wound up another gear and drove straight at their sneering faces—seeing nothing but the bloodshot hunger in their eyes.

SIX

"**N**ow who in his right—" Kelly choked over his words. He spoked his fingers across the back of his head. He stretched his chest and held his breath for half a minute before he let air pass over his teeth.

"I wound up my top gear. I didn't care." He tried to speak again, his voice broken and stained with anger. "I stood up and attacked them—charged right through the middle of those greasy, obese—that's what they were, too—fat, slobbering—" He glared into the grass between his legs, his eyes loose and rushing.

"What happened after that?" Roberto asked, motioning to Fowler to get Kelly a mug of apple cider.

"A lot of rifle cracks went off behind me. Sounded like they were shooting over my head.

Then, that was it. Got totally quiet back there."

Trying to relax his breathing, trying to relax the tension in his face, Kelly punched Huffman on the arm. "One of them had red splotches on his face. Those were gin blossoms. I figured it out the second time through the line."

"They could've porked you a few good ones. Chopped you up, dug you under the ground back up in there," Huffman said. He snatched the cider out of Fowler's hand, splashing most of it into the grass, and passed the dripping mug to Kelly.

"I'm sure if I'd eased to a stop, asked them to help me find a new route back to the park, they'd have driven me—to a pizza parlor. But they provoked me. I provoked them right back. They provoked me right back, and we all went nuts. And this isn't the first time I've done something like that."

His memory deepened the tone of his voice. "About two years ago, I pulled up to a stop sign back near my house. I was minding my own business, waiting for a pick-up truck to pass. Two guys in the back tossed firecrackers on me."

Kelly put his empty mug beside him in the grass and squeezed his hands together. "Same thing went off inside of me. I was up in a sprint, chasing that truck. The driver saw me coming back there and hit the brakes. They all three jumped out, pulled me off my bike. Caught me in a cross fire."

"And the headline reads, strange cleat marks bloody faces of three dead men," Roberto said.

"Never got the chance, Ro. One slugged me in the back of the head. I turned around, the two other thugs kicked me in the back. They cut my lips open, beat me in the chest—they really did a job on one of my ribs. I had trouble breathing and sleeping for a wee—"

"You've got to quit riding these things!" Blount tensed his fists—tensed the muscles in his neck. "Do this long enough—it's just a matter of time before one of you gets yourself good and smashed up."

Laying the weight of his cinder-block eyes on Kelly, he said, "I didn't say anything earlier, but when I came up behind you Friday on Sixteen, cars were swooshing by you—seventy, seventy-five easily." He pointed a broken stick at Kelly, then at Burkhart. "Most didn't slow down. It's not like their mother or best friend's out there on that road. I'd say they were annoyed at you for being in their way, not to mention that can somebody hurled at you."

Huffman struck his fist into his open palm. "So I loved that motor home that pushed on me."

More like tried to scalp him. Nothing happened and Fowler kept it to himself—in frustration, in confusion—in part because he figured Huffman would have to beat him out of it, at least in his own mind, if he did say something, but he saw that RV shave so close on him, the side-view mirror cut right over the top of his helmet.

"You can bet on one thing—one thing's been decided," Huffman said. "I'm going to get him back. He's going to be good and sorry he messed with me after I get done with his tires. And windshield."

Burkhart used Huffman's shoulder to push himself up. "For one thing, no one needs to be driving no house," he said, looking at the road that bent its way into the dark and silent woods.

"Well, obviously a lot of people are trying to tell you no one has any business riding a bicycle out there either," Blount said.

"Check the donor list for ears, furball. I'm telling you. Those lane blimps don't even fit into a normal l-ane. And that's another thing, right there. Bikes don't make the air stink like somebody's cooking d-irty underwear."

Still glaring at the empty road—still, in his nagging contempt, trying to deny any truth to what Blount had said, Burkhart cocked more anger on his tongue. "Look at who drives those ego trips. Hey, I called on this, too. They don't have to pass no test, they don't have to get no special license, they don't have to log no training hours, like truckers—hey, this is America. No matter how big the rig, just pay the bucks, and off you go to flop all over the animals and the b-ikes."

He tossed his water bottle down in front of him and chewed at a loose piece of skin on his lower lip.

"They think they're pioneers or something because they wheeze themselves two whole inches out of their roly-poly homes and gardens and fry animal parts on a grill."

Not saying anything for almost a minute, he made a grumbling sound like water boiling, his eyes tracing the sky along the western trees. Then, he turned his scowling face on Blount. "Like that makes him t-ough, or bigger on the f-ood chain, besides the fact he gets big bird and the horn of plenty on every bridge, every no-passing zone, every—hey, he gets himself kicked—now he's got to p-ass it on down the line."

"I read that the Italians treat their bike racers like gods," Fowler said. He mumbled his words into his hands, recognizing the futility in what he was trying to say. But it was no kidding. Instead of getting violent, the Italians slow down. That's because they worship their bike racers. They want to give them food and money. "They want to honk and wave."

"I'm telling you something here," Burkhart said.

"They honk at us in America. With their middle fingers. They honk with their middle f-ingers, their front bumpers, their beer cans, their freaking zero IQs. But hey, you ain't seen no honkies yet. You wait till it gets cold, and they catch you out here in tights."

Fowler felt defeated, not sad but hurt, his shoulders rounding from the weight of his frustration. "I was riding alone last year. Somebody came up behind me. The guy with him reached out the window—he tried to grab me," he mumbled again, rubbing his chin as if he'd like to wipe off the memory. "I'm sorry, that's creepy. Feeling that guy's hand on my back."

"See, right there it is." Burkhart crowbarred himself back in like Fowler hadn't bothered to say anything. "That bouncing bully goes and springs a building on a nineteen pound bike—hey, we got the fat man out here dancing on strawberries."

He yanked his water bottle out of the grass at his feet. "I guarantee you he's got about enough brains to fall asleep in his wussy-boy recliner five whole seconds after he mangles a cow for dinner."

"We've been lucky with this team so far," Kelly said. He stood up and patted Burkhart on the shoulder, but for all his intended kindness, he looked like he'd just reached into the toxic space of a cornered rat.

He tried to speak again, to find affirmation. "But we should stop pushing that luck, riding on roads where cars could tailbone us at—"

"I don't agree with any of this," Blount shouted over Kelly. "Gush all you want about how people should and shouldn't do this and that—I'm just telling you what you need to hear about the world you really live in. You're nothing more to those people out there than a cockroach on the side of the road."

He glared at Kelly, then at Burkhart, the wind splashing in the trees above his head. "Cars and bikes don't mix. Who's riding home with me in the Windstar?"

SEVEN

Fowler's house was dark when he pedaled his
bike into the driveway at six-thirty. His father
worked late hours setting up his newest chain of
restaurants, not getting home sometimes till one or
two in the morning. His mother didn't work, but
when the house was dark like this, Fowler knew
she'd been sleeping all afternoon. Sleeping and
drinking.

He pushed his bike into the blackened foyer and
felt his way down the hall to his room. Halfway
through the door, he hesitated, running his hand
along the inside of the wall. He struck the light
switch like a match, and his mind flamed with
memories.

In the bright room, he sat on his bed, fingering
through pictures of his friends in Pittsburgh. like
this one kid named Boots, dressed in this baggy

lion's suit he had rented to trick-or-treat one year at Halloween. His mind wandered back to the day Boots managed to unplug one of the hoses on his mother's washing machine. It flooded the laundry room and half of Fowler's kitchen before they could wade behind the thing and turn off the water. No telling how he did it, but another time he pulled the fireplace mantle off the wall in Fowler's living room. That was one looney kid, that Boots.

Fowler looked at the picture of the tree fort—more like the cross between a hammock and the deck of a Spanish galleon—he and Boots built one summer. He remembered how they had picked through this junk yard on the street behind the fire station. For two weeks, they hauled warped lumber, a bag of nails, sheets of yellowed linoleum, tar paper, shingles, and rope a good mile to the top of this hill. It was the greatest thing—building that deck—sailing a million miles over the city—over the rest of the world—in that Sleepy Hollow tree.

Fowler crossed the new mauve carpet in his bedroom. He had called Boots a lot since he moved.

At first, they talked like old times—about school, about parents, about Fowler's old friends—but when Boots got a car, he was either never home or always had somewhere he had to go. He said he'd call back. But he never did.

In the lamp light over his desk, Fowler punched Boots's numbers into his phone. He heard the spaced alarms, sparking their way to Pittsburgh. He pushed the receiver back into its cradle, his face wet across his forehead.

He turned over another picture. Boots had found a box full of pulleys and nylon cord and had rigged a device to hoist Fowler's dog up onto the hammock floor.

Fowler punched Boots's numbers again.

He looked at his watch. The house was still tombstone silent. He knew his mother hadn't eaten anything all day.

You're the only one who cares about me, he remembered his mother saying when she broke her arm, and Fowler made her breakfast, lunch, and dinner for a week. He was ten. It was summer, during a heat wave that kept daytime temperatures in the high nineties. His mother complained that she couldn't leave the house, but Fowler knew it was just another dodge to flood the holes in her life with whiskey, gin, and constant vodka.

He opened his bedroom door and slipped back into the dark house. He felt his way again down the hall and into the blackened foyer. He painted the wall with his hand, stroking for the kitchen and dining room light switches beside the foyer door.

Braiding his fingers, pressing his elbows against his ribs, he moved across the white tile and stepped onto the green carpet in the living room.

He pulled the cold brass chain of a table lamp and stared at his mother, lying in her blue sink of a couch on the other side of the room.

"Mom?" Fowler sputtered.

In her youth, Marissa Applegate had been a musician. She had blossomed with the keys of her piano into a bright and vital world all her own. Fowler had found newspaper clippings one day when he was digging through the linen closet for some shoe polish. They were buried under hand towels in the bottom of a dusty box.

The young woman in the clippings didn't look like his mother. She looked confident. She looked bold. She looked like she could fly.

His mother pursued her gift for three years at Julliard, mystifying audiences in New York, Boston, Pittsburgh, Philadelphia, and Baltimore with her touch, with her voice.

But then she stopped playing. With no explanation to her parents—with no warnings to her professors—she stopped playing altogether.

Fowler had done some guessing. Like how she told him once he was just in her way—that she had never wanted him to live.

He had asked about the piano in the living room, never getting more than a shrug, but when he asked about the clippings, his mother scolded him never to question the decisions she made for herself.

A few nights later, Fowler heard her coursing through Brahms's CAPRICCIO IN C-SHARP MINOR—her voice high and pitching, spilling out of her like the light of a full moon.

He had never heard his mother play. Not before that night. He could feel her rising out of the house—journeying to some un-named part of the world deep inside herself. She wasn't playing a piano. She was talking to God.

At first, he lay motionless under his blanket, transfixed by the person awakened in the bright notes. He climbed out of bed and moused his way down the hall, closer to the piano—closer to the mother he had never met before.

But the music stopped. As suddenly as it had begun, it stopped. Fowler descended the darkened stairs, gripping the banister with each step, and hesitated at the living room carpet. "Mom?" he called into the silence. But his mother sat frozen at her instrument.

Fowler was eleven years old. He didn't know what to say. He didn't know what to think. He was only eleven, and he didn't know what to do.

Now, four years later, he still didn't know what to do.

"Mom?" he sputtered again at the shadow on the blue couch. "Mom, can you get up now?"

He crossed the room and touched his mother's arm. As if bitten, his mother flinched—jerked her arm away.

"Mom, you've got to eat," Fowler said. He rooted his hands under his mother's head.

"Get your shitty hands off me."

"Come on in the kitchen. It's getting really late," Fowler urged, struggling to pull his mother up.

"I hate you, Colby."

"Now you know that's the vodka talking and not—"

Marissa dug her fingernails into Fowler's face. She dug with vicious strength—hard and pitiless—scratching, clawing at Fowler's cheek—ripping channels of blood from his ear to his lips.

Fowler recoiled. He jumped away from his mother. He shrieked and stepped farther back into the room. He heard a buzzing noise in his ears and found himself running toward the kitchen. His skin pulsed—it caught fire—and he pulled a palm of blood away from his face.

In the kitchen, he snatched for a box of raisin bran and three bananas. He clutched a bottle of spring water to his chest and ran again toward his room.

He unrolled his sleeping bag onto his bed and hurried across the hall to the bathroom. Straining at the waist, stretching himself over the top of the white-marbled vanity, Fowler looked into the mirror at his violated face. With trembling hands, he washed his cheek and striped Polysporin into the tracks left by his mother's fingernails.

Back in his own room, he rolled his toothbrush and a half tube of Crest into his sleeping bag. He stuffed his backpack with clean riding shorts and jerseys, riding socks, his wind jacket, school clothes, his bananas, cereal, school books, and two hundred dollars he'd been stockpiling to go back to Pittsburgh. He filled two red bottles with water, caged them onto his bike, tied his sleeping bag onto the top of his backpack, and pushed his bike back down the hall to the foyer door.

EIGHT

The balcony in front of Kelly's classroom cut off the bitter night wind that followed Fowler back to school.

He tried not to think about his mother, lying back there in that blue coffin.

She's a psycho, he said to himself and pawed his two hundred dollars out of his backpack. Forty, maybe fifty bucks, he thought, fingering through a few tens and twenties. All he'd need is food—stuff like cereal, dates, bananas, broccoli, baked chicken —he could get all that at grocery stores. Ditch his backpack and tie his sleeping bag onto his handlebars, like he'd seen in the bike magazines. A hundred miles a day easy, sleeping in the woods back off the roads. But he wouldn't call Boots.

His stomach burned. He wished he had brought a loaf of bread to soak up the acid. To soak up his mother's violence.

It's the meanest thing, he thought. Like she was always picking fights with his dad. She'd hit him with this blizzard of accusations. Then, if he tried to apologize, to reason with her, to correct a mistake—do something about what she just got done bludgeoning him for—then, he got the guilt hatchet. Like this one Christmas eve. She started ordering him to take her home—back to her birth and childhood farm in Bethlehem. It was eleven o'clock at night. Fowler's whole world stopped breathing right there in that living room.

His dad told him it was just the alcohol talking. But blowing up a family like that on Christmas eve. That kept him thinking. Not until tonight did he piece together the red welts and bleeding scratches he had seen on his dad's forearm. At the time, he hadn't asked about them. He figured his dad had grabbed one of the family cats for peeing in the ficus tree planter beside the foyer door. It was one of the family cats, all right. And her claws spoke from the mainspring of her rabid behavior, right up there with that black vodka.

It's one thing to hate somebody's guts. But that's sick what she did—digging those fingernails into somebody's skin like that.

It got Fowler thinking. He had never seen his mother smile. Not at him at least. Not even out in public when she had to lug him to the store or to the doctor. But she was sure smiling when she dug her nails into his cheek—a dark brilliance, hard and ancient, passing through her eyes the moment she got her sting into his face. Pay-back for tripping over him for fifteen years.

It's so unfair, he thought. He ate his bananas and some dry cereal and searched through the wrought iron railing into the lighted courtyard below.

His mind wandered, and he remembered the training ride the day before they left for Gold Head State Park—he remembered Huffman's beagle-puppy eyes, how he had tried to snivel Kelly into packing his guitar for the trip.

About this hayride in your dreams. Try a stress test if Roberto shows up, Kelly had teased, as they rode their bikes toward Brooks Hall and into the courtyard, glowing in the copper light of the evening sun. And do us all a favor, Huffman. Get lots of extra sleep tonight so we don't have to tow your boiling wabinga around all weekend.

Unrolling his sleeping bag, Fowler hesitated, his vision pulled up to Kelly's classroom door. Taped to the weathered doorknob was the picture of a lion sleeping under a tree in the African veldt. Burkhart, he thought. Burkhart's face stalled in his memory. That cold-rock frown he always drove between himself and Fowler.

He stared at the ragged green trees beyond the courtyard, the silence rising up around them like the fog, thick without exception.

He thought about the fog that steamed out of the hills behind his house in Pittsburgh. He remembered this old man who lived back up in there. He looked like a ghost—white hair and a long white beard.

Kids were bragging one day at school that the old man had shot them full of rock salt when they went poking around his house. Of course, Boots had to try it for himself, so he and Fowler and two other boys met one Friday afternoon at the dirt road that cut its way up into the trees like a comb.

They kept passing no trespassing signs—so many of them Fowler lost count—and other warnings about condemned property. But that old man lived back in there, all right. They crouched awhile in the grass that blew like long fur in the acre field that fronted the two-story house—more like someone had tried to frame an old farm house with unpainted barn wood.

He wasn't there. The old man had this wagon he drove to the stores at the bottom of the hill, and the wagon was gone. So Boots stood up and beat his way through the grass right up to the front door. Fowler yelled at him, but he wouldn't listen.

Nothing happened. He just kept standing there, so Fowler and the two other boys crept up onto the porch.

The place had no glass in the windows. It smelled like urine inside, and the floors were covered with empty food cans—all of them for dogs and cats. But there weren't any dogs or cats up there, and the old man always came down the hill alone.

And that was it. No wagon, no shotguns, no ghost. But Boots went back to school Monday morning blustering about how the old man had shot his tail off. He had poked holes in a pair of jeans and kept pulling them out of his locker between periods. Fowler never found out where he got it, but he kept sticking out a hand full of rock salt, too. Bloody rock salt.

Fowler burrowed into his sleeping bag and stared back at Burkhart's paper lion, caught like Kelly's locked door in the quiet flow of the night.

Nothing ever changed.

He pulled his legs tighter against his stomach, bleeding now deep inside his intestines. He pressed the sleeve of his jersey into the leaks in his eyes.

NINE

S tudents began to stir Monday afternoon, laughing and shouting on the balcony in front of Kelly's second-story classroom door. Kelly's next class followed a full one-hour break for lunch when everyone was allowed to wander through the long islands of umbrella oaks that sailed their branches over the Coleman campus, or along the grassy banks of the river.

Juniors and seniors often sat in pairs, or in small groups, recovering from the grinding challenges of morning classes in physics, calculus, chemistry, Western civilization, and literature. Younger students were more magnetic—less bitter, less worn and irritable than their older peers.

Kelly heard a soft tapping, and then Fowler slipped into his room. He looked bent and hurt. In his own class at ten, he had looked tired. Now, he looked frightened. And pale.

"I know you have class and stuff." Fowler looked at Kelly with uncertain vision. "But can—can you talk to me for a few minutes?"

"Sure," Kelly said. "Here, sit in my favorite chair, which just so happens to be my only chair."

Missing Kelly's attempt at cheering him up—showing no response at all—Fowler stared at the face of Richard Cory hanging ashen on the wall.

Kelly opened his door and told a few students to spread the word that class would begin a bit late—to be quiet and please not to make him come out to settle anyone down. When he returned to his room, Fowler was sitting, silently toying with his fingers in his lap. Perhaps the angle of light hit him more directly, more intensely now, but he looked pale as white marble, at least around his eyes.

Feeling a tightening in his chest and throat, Kelly pulled the shades over the balcony windows and door, sensing that, more than any other time in his life, Fowler needed privacy and not the busy politics of his curious peers. Kelly had never seen anyone so dejected and tired.

"Are you—ok?" he said, not sure what to say, if anything.

Fowler didn't respond at first. He seemed not even to have heard Kelly's hesitant question. Then, he shrugged his shoulders and stared at him, ceramic white and cold.

The tight feeling in Kelly's throat grew painful, and the room began to swirl around him. He paced back and forth in front of Fowler. Something gnawed at him to speak, but his mouth was filled with heavy rocks.

"I can't—" Fowler stopped his breath through his trembling lips and dropped his head to one side. "I—I don't want to live anymore."

The room shrank. The air got hard to breathe. Kelly turned to the shaded door so that Fowler wouldn't have to endure the shock in his eyes.

Half turning in his chair, Fowler groped with stumbling, uncertain fingers for the sleeve of Kelly's shirt.

"Did something happen to you when you got

home last night?" Kelly asked, pointing to the white bandage on Fowler's cheek.

"Here." Fowler picked one end of the bandage loose and let it hang off his jaw. "Here's what I get for trying to feed my mother." When he tried to explain, tears swelled his eyes. He reached to catch his lower lip. "I'm sorry, Coach—I'm really sorry for this."

Kelly knelt down beside him—faltered—pawed for his shoulder. "What're you going to do?"

Fowler gulped back the muscles jumping in his throat. "I've got two hundred dollars in my pocket," he said. "I can go back to Pittsburgh. Of course, nobody can remember who I am up there either. Or I can buy a can of Drano."

"You can't run away from this."

"Easy for you to say." Fowler twisted his hands until the ends of his fingers darkened.

"I grew up with a guy who had good reasons not to feel wanted." Trying to relax his breathing, trying to relax the tension, the heaviness in his chest, Kelly kept tapping at the arm of Fowler's chair. "He had all the skis, tennis rackets, golf clubs, records, transistor radios, switch-blade knives he ever asked for—some new gadget every week. But he didn't have anybody to talk to. He wasn't even allowed to eat with his parents. They said he made them nervous. And to keep him out of their way, they hired a nurse, a live-in, full-time nurse to take care of him, so they didn't have to."

Kelly pinched a piece of wet grass off Fowler's shoe. "Well, one day he started drinking, carrying a flask. He got so hooked on escaping his own shadow, so lonely, so good and dead inside, he couldn't get out of bed in the morning without a zonk or two of vodka. He was an alcoholic by the time he was fourteen, Fowler. It got so bad one night after a party, he couldn't get his key into his front door. The people who claimed to be his friends made sure he got good and drunk. They thought he was perfectly hilarious. And the more they laughed, the zanier he got. He was Pavlov's booze-dog. Dive through any hoop, do any woozy-boozy trick to get those heads turning his way."

"Like what? Like what did he start doing?" Fowler stretched his hands around the back of his head.

"Well, like urinating down laundry shoots. Swinging on chandeliers. Crazy stuff like lying in the street at night when a car was coming, and giving people hell rides in his GTO, that fire-engine red muscle car his parents bought him on his sixteenth birthday. I tried to tell him where he was heading, but he had to wreck that hot rod—break three of his ribs, cut half his date's face off, and paralyze her left arm—before he started seeing it for himself."

Fowler stood up and walked to the unshaded windows that faced the lush football field toward the entrance to the school. He pointed at the rolls of clouds steaming over the blue and gold bleachers and press box, but something else caught his eye. A great blue heron broke out of a line of thick magnolia trees at the lower end of the parking lot. The huge bird swung low, flying with cathedral stillness over the city of empty cars.

"After that wreck—" Kelly paused. He stood beside Fowler now and leaned against the window. "This guy didn't even touch a beer for over three months. But people said he wasn't any fun anymore. If he tried to sit with them at lunch, these jerks would either ignore him or leave the table. Now this guy is never talked to at home, and all of a sudden he's getting the silent treatment at school. You can't work blind in a jungle of quicksand."

Kelly shook his head. "Off he went to another drinking party. Now do you happen to know what goes on inside an alcoholic who takes a drink after going dry for three months? He goes nuts. The grave diggers thought it would be hilarious to see him do doughnuts around the fountain in front of the country club, so they poured him into the second new red GTO his parents got him the day after he totaled the first one. They poured him into that car—poured him like the bottles of beer, whiskey, gin, and vodka they had poured down his throat all night. Yep, he did their sick doughnut trick. He gave them another buzz, too—one they weren't expecting. He laid rubber down the half-mile driveway. Hit an oak tree at redline in third gear."

"Did he die?" Fowler asked.

"Came out of it with this." Kelly ran his finger down a scar on his neck.

A row of ceiling lights ached into the silent room. They leeched like the blood draining out of Fowler's ears.

"Time is your best friend, Fowler. I'm the living witness. You have a future beyond your mother."

Fowler slid away from the window and dropped into Kelly's swivel chair, his shirt wet and cold, stinging his back between his shoulder blades and just above his belt.

"Right now, go crank up that Pinarello buddy of yours and meet me down in the courtyard"—Kelly swung him in the direction of the door—"in five minutes."

He looked up with surprise. He said, "Coach, you can't—"

"Meter's running, wild man."

Kelly was risking a lot of heat with this one.

Coleman Academy operated on do-or-die policy, and MacLaughlin could fire a teacher for calling off class like this, for not sending Fowler to the counseling office. But Kelly wasn't just talking. He wasn't kidding.

A new glimmer reddened Fowler's face. Boots knew stuff—he knew the drill with his mother—but he couldn't talk to Boots. Not like this.

"Some day maybe you can pull your own boiling wabinga around this county," Fowler said. He loosened his grip on the arm of the chair and stood up. "Ok, let's get thrown out of Coleman together, right?"

"I hear Episcopal's looking for someone to start a bike team. And you can visit me in jail."

Fowler's eyes brightened—his head nodding in wonder and appreciation. "You don't have to...kidnap me."

"Come back if you need kidnapped. Or call me tonight. Call me any night. I'm serious, Fowler. No matter how late it gets."

"Thanks," Fowler said with more color

streaming into his face. "I won't forget this."

TEN

Fowler felt drained by the clamor of students pushing and shoving their way along the narrow balcony in front of Kelly's classroom. The noise, the thunder—bodies trampling over each other, yelling like no one could hear.

He gripped the brass rail at the edge of the balcony, feeling the cold and knotted world crawling back under his skin.

The students disappeared into Kelly's room, and Fowler walked alone in the silence to the top of the stairs. He hesitated. The steps looked like the keys on his mother's piano, sinking into the dark stairwell.

His stomach tightened. He steadied his head in the palms of his hands and fixed his eyes back on Kelly's door. He didn't wish he had never been born.

ELEVEN

"**C**rank it up, Fowler!" Kelly shouted Saturday morning, trying to heat up interval training.

"It feels like someone's trying to rip something out of my back!"

"Maybe one of these days you'll get around to bending those telephone-pole elbows of yours!" Kelly tried not to sound disappointed, even sarcastic, but revealed his frustration over the reluctant pace.

"Twenty-nine, twenty-eight to go, Fowler! Don't make me push you! Push yourself! Twenty more seconds now! Nineteen! Eighteen! Come on, man! Un-hitch that Winnebago! Burkhart's already snoring back here!"

Intervals might be mistaken for self-torture, every rider at some point asking why anyone would take—and keep taking—this much pain, except that no other kind of training more effectively develops an ability to endure the constant jockeying for position, the surges, pack sprints, attacks, breakaways, and chases of actual racing.

The interval rider can't just take a turn at the front. He has to dig at maximum heart rate—surge as hard as he can—surge in anaerobic violence—torment himself for one, two, or three hellish minutes. And then slip to the rear of the paceline.

Forced now into the vulnerable position of having to catch the last wheel of the training group, where he can't get the full sucking effect of being surrounded by other riders—having to work harder to chase surges once he does hitch onto the rear of the pack—or worse, being whip-lashed through the turns—he faces the second most demanding challenge of interval training.

Already tired—maybe even dizzy—his bike feeling heavy and wobbling under him—cranking in what's called the no-man's land—now he's got to reinspire his lungs and muscular resources in order not to get dropped, in order not to get shelled off the back, in order not to get blown out of the training ride altogether.

"The Germans call these things fart-licks." Huffman guffawed under his breath.

"Hardly the same emphasis you're trying to put on that word," Kelly said with his usual inflections of warning and yet patient support. "And the word's fartlek."

That was a funny-sounding word, all right. But a real one. Fowler had checked it with the German teacher at Coleman. He thought it came from fahrtstrecke, meaning interval.

"So you can bet your boiling wabinga—"

"Keep milking it, Huffman." Kelly motioned to break from the grinding work. "You just keep on milking it. Now, since you like these things so much, I've got a bit of news for you. We're going to let you get us started on phase two."

Huffman's eyes took over his whole face. "Phase two?"

"I was brushing my teeth this morning, thinking about you, Huffman. Thinking how in this convoluted world you're going to ride your bike today with no legs."

On the last training ride, Huffman kept whining how Kelly was putting the hurt on this bike team—meaning himself, of course—turning every training ride into a mock race.

Only way you learn how to race, Kelly had said, is—you got it—to race. Fowler didn't know what Kelly was up to this time, but he could hear the chain saw puttering.

"Not that I didn't hear you offer to pay Burkhart to take your pulls five miles out. But there I was, brushing my teeth, trying to figure out how you could find your legs in time to ride today—when powee, out of nowhere, a dog rang my doorbell. Yep, there sat a dog, Huffman. A golden retriever named Phase Two."

Kelly was good at catching the difference between burn-out, or danger signs that could lead to injury or depression, and Huffman's politics or attempted manipulation. Thanks to the psycho's last journey off the path, Kelly had the whole team firing on what he liked to call the one-arm-whammy, some maniacal pushup he'd seen Sylvester Stallone doing in ROCKY, with one arm forced half way up his back.

"And Phase Two said—now, this is what he said, Huffman. I'm not changing a single word of this. He said he was out hammering down Old Mandarin Road this morning, and he, and he—" Kelly struggled to get something out of the pocket in his jersey.

"See, here they are." Kelly jiggled two plastic GI Joe legs on a string over the top of Huffman's handlebars. "Yep, a golden dog retrieved your legs. Snatched them right out of the middle of the road, right where we took these two little wheel suckers off for you yesterday."

Squeaking, trying to talk but half choking, half gulping, Huffman closed his hand over the plastic legs.

"Now that's some bike racer's dream dog, that

Phase Two."

"Can somebody please tell me why you always do this every time you're up to something rotten?" Burkhart said. "No, we aren't sore enough from your freaking—hey, I've got something to guarantee you. He's cooked up some new way to torture us."

"On the coils of the Wood Kelly leg burning stove—you see, we're going to heat up the interval work. Everything else stays the same, guys. Just exactly what we've been doing. We're just tossing this extra who-loves-ya-log on the fire. Huffman, you get to go first. Cut your speed to fifteen, count off thirty slow seconds, then sprint and chase us. If you catch us, bene fatto. If you don't, best thing that could happen to you. It'll make you mad. You'll work harder for once, strengthen yourself more each week. Fowler, you're next, then Burkhart. I go las—"

"You'd better put the plug in this one till later, Coach!" Fowler waved his hand over one shoulder and then the other. "We've got two Torcoletties coming at us back here!"

"Take the front, Huffman!" Kelly pushed at Huffman's back. "Echelon the draft to the right! Tie up as much of the road as you can!" he shouted to everyone.

Fowler and Burkhart sailed like Canadian geese into formation behind Huffman.

"Get on them now—right when they deal on us!" Kelly kept shouting. "Then, stay in tight! They'll rock as soon as they catch open road!"

"It's Blankenship and Crell!" Fowler shouted back.

TWELVE

Kelly shot ahead of Huffman and Burkhart, swinging like a wrecking ball for Crell's rear wheel.

The fiery jerseys dodged to the opposite side of the road.

Kelly countered the attack—snapping himself like stretched elastic back into Crell's draft.

He surged to his left to block more crosswind.

Crell drove against Kelly's front wheel—he cut across his line—he cut for open asphalt—Blankenship sprinting straight ahead to manipulate the breakaway attempt.

One—two more dodges—to the left—to the right, and the Torcoletti team locked back together on the far side of the solid-yellow center line—Kelly sprinting over the gap—attacking Crell's position—attacking Crell.

Sweat stung Kelly's eyes and dripped like blown glass from the ends of his nose and chin. He tasted rust—on his tongue—deep in his throat.

He burst out of his saddle again—digging and pulling at his pedals—breaking a few meters away from the two engines—chuffing for his back.

THIRTEEN

Ashby Crell and Kevin Blankenship raced for
Team Torcoletti. Team sponsor Silvio
Torcoletti, a wizard with legs and knees and bicycle
parts, had been loading these two young pistols for
three years with the physics and the politics of
bicycle racing.

For all his exaggerations, Torcoletti really did
know more about bicycle racing than anyone else in
Northeast Florida. He really had drafted Eddy
Merckx for about ten miles during Paris-Roubaix,
and he really had roped himself a position in a six-
man breakaway group that went down to the finish
line that same year in one stage of the Giro d'Italia,
two achievements he recited like prayers to
everyone who spoke to him. But despite the
honesty of his success, the dream that he could win
even one stage of a world tour chased him every

day and night of his life, until at the age of thirty-nine he sailed for America, intending to win his race through the young riders he could find and mesmerize in a country just struggling to its feet with a new sport. Fourteen years later, on the threshold of being impounded by a Chapter Thirteen at the small shop where he sold and repaired bicycles for a living, he was laying all his psychic bets on Blankenship and Crell.

Sweat flew off the side of Crell's head, flattening into the skin wrinkled over the knuckle of Kelly's thumb. "We could do this all the way to Hastings!" Kelly shouted in broken syllables to the two bright jerseys swarming in front of him.

"I see Roberto finally wised up and dumped you all," Crell called back, easing his strokes, trying to look and sound untousled, as if he'd just climbed out of a great shower—trying to lick and seal his pride into an impudent tone so that no one—certainly not Kelly—might suspect he had suffered any loss of power or dignity through the violence of the competition moments ago.

"Not at all—just had to work again." Kelly struggled to speak with his lungs still trying to force their way out of his mouth. "Come on back and hammer with us today. Make them ride harder. I'm about to switch them over to chases."

"Now that's a boring idea. You see, I'm not as interested as you are, man, in ruining my training day on an elephant walk. It makes a whole lot more sense for you to run with us. But you can tell Burkhart he can kiss my ass when he gets old enough to ride a bike."

"You're talking to yourself, Crell," Kelly grumbled, already half way through his turn back down County Road Thirteen.

FOURTEEN

Still grumbling, Kelly crossed the Julington Creek Bridge and centered his weight for the turn back onto Old Mandarin Road. Two hundred meters ahead of the first line of banner oaks, Burkhart came soaring toward him—soaring and screaming, his voice deafening, desperate, as soon as he caught sight of Kelly.

"I could've held that attack if I had someone like Torcoletti giving me real b-ikes."

He chewed at his lips and reached for his brake levers. "Here, you try it yourself. This junkyard drop of flapping blue jays. I'm jamming a freaking waterbed at high t-ide."

"Quit shifting the blame," Kelly laughed, squirting Burkhart in the chest with red Gatorade.

"Can I ride your b-ike?" Burkhart blew another gasket, seeing Huffman storming into view.

"You won't go any faster."

"Oh sure, you can say that. Your frame cost more than my whole f-reaking—ok, ok, those wheels. Give me five—no, two and a half miles. I drop you—I keep the wheels."

"Better throw a Harley on them."

"You're against me."

"Not at all. We keep telling you, Burkhart. You're fighting yourself."

Burkhart shrugged his shoulders.

"All that mind candy you keep buying. You've gobbled up enough inventory to open your own bike shop." Kelly squirted Burkhart with more Gatorade. "Have you found one second of speed for all that labor and expense? Have you made any new whirlwind of a bike go any faster than any older one?"

Huffman and Fowler stroked now in back of Burkhart. Only the sound of their chains and tires pulled up the road behind them.

Kelly glanced at his watch and smiled back at Burkhart. "Do you think it ever crossed your buddy

Indurain's mind that he couldn't hold a break or win the Tour de France unless he had a Look or a Time or Kestrel fork? Or a Zipp this or Zap that?"

"Ok, ok—but how am I supposed to find out what helps me if I don't try everything first?"

"Trying things with a clear head—that's one thing, Burkhart. But that's not what you're doing. You're only feeding the outside of this sport. Advertisers suck you into believing you're not a complete bike racer until you buy the stuff that got some big boy over the line, and off you go driving Pennington nuts."

Kelly flagged his hand in front of Burkhart's simpering face. "Can't you see the contradiction in that kind of thinking? Or lack of thinking."

A cyclone of defenses stormed in Burkhart's eyes, but he still just humped his shoulders up and down.

"So what happened? So where are they? They drop you?" Huffman pleaded, shattering Kelly's attention as if he had tossed pieces of broken glass in front of his tires.

"No, but not because they didn't throw everything in bicycle history at me. They ride like the Italians. All that hollow-point stuff Torcoletti loads into them. They fired it. They fired it at me. At least a dozen times."

Kelly tinkered with his helmet strap. "I got ahead of them twice," he said. "But they really do work well together, so they just spun me back into their web. Every time I tried to cut them in half—huh, they knew all about that game, and just kept blocking and surging, or dodging all over the road. So, the only way I got to draft was on the whiplash. Ho, ho, ho, ho, ho—and did they ever whip my lashes."

He rubbed his hand back and forth across his lips until they reddened. "And my lungs. I could taste them. It felt like I was breathing them out of my mouth."

That one got Fowler thinking—Kelly's lungs hanging off his handlebars—shivering yellow and white, dripping onto his front tire.

"I can now tell you how it feels to sweat

eyeballs," Kelly said. "Yep, I could see the look on Torcoletti's face when he found my eyeballs and pieces of my forehead stuck on the back of Crell's jer—"

Huffman slapped his thigh and shouted over Kelly, "So what happened?"

"Well, ok, if you don't want to hear about my eyeballs. A few miles down Thirteen, nothing had changed, so I asked them to come back and train with us. Crell wasn't too thrilled with that idea. Wasn't too friendly either, guys."

"So at least he talks," Huffman said. Anger and impatience pulled sharp edges across his mouth. "That Blankenship, he's the real fairy. Makes you nervous. So you never know what he's up to."

Fowler's eyes danced. He knew something—a secret about Blankenship. "He's nice when you get him alone," he said.

He had seen Blankenship at a movie, and they sat together. It was about this man who takes care of his father. He had this circulation problem in his legs, or something that rotted his feet. Blankenship all of a sudden told Fowler he saw his father so drunk one night he couldn't get him off the floor of his front porch. He said he started to lift him up. But his pants felt wet from his crotch clear down to his knees.

When Fowler asked him what he did next, he might have been crying or something because he just shrugged his shoulders and looked the other way. Not even at the screen.

Fowler could feel his tires shuddering over the nervous cracks in the road.

He remembered one day he was at a friend's house. He was supposed to leave at five, but his mother still hadn't come two hours after she said she'd pick him up. His friend's mom was nice, but she kept asking if he was staying for dinner. It kept getting later and later, so he called. He could hear his mother squealing on the other end of the telephone line. There was a lot of shrill laughing in the background, and he could hear his aunt and a bunch of his mother's friends who used to come over a lot. He just—he just kept asking his mother if she was going to come for him. He didn't know what else to say.

Wind rushed at Fowler's ears. He pulled in behind Kelly and trembled under his chin.

His friend's sister—he had no idea she was on the other line. She heard most of it. She told her parents something like his mother was drunk and falling on the floor. Well, she was drunk, all right, and slurring her words, but she didn't fall. She dropped the phone on a table and knocked over some glasses. But his friend's mom wanted to believe the worst, and he was never allowed to play or spend the night at Corbin's house again.

"So I wish we had shirts like that," Huffman said. "Those are really cool shirts," he dripped, trying to make everybody look at him. Some of his teachers at Coleman thought Huffman had Attention Deficit Disorder, but Fowler knew better. He just liked to filch attention. This kid wouldn't give a dried rat's leg for somebody else's feelings.

"So how about that same red and yellow zig-zagging stuff," he kept harping. "Good stuff, huh?

And all those little things that look like paint splashes all over the place? Or they might be fireworks. And wait, wait—Coach, we can put–"

"Now, Coach," Burkhart cut in, making a noise with his tongue that sounded like somebody clicking at a dog. "Is the Big Mac paying for uniforms?"

Headmaster MacLaughlin chirped around campus like Ronald McDonald. He was also huge—towering six feet, eight and a half inches—and shaped like the Philadelphia bell from his chest to his belly, so everyone called him Big Mac.

"We're on our own for a little while longer."

"The freaking c-heeseburger!" Burkhart's anger burned red across his face. "Eight coaches—hey, golf carts, new helmets every year, a new stadium—and he can't find two bills for our s-hirts."

"The trustees and boosters want football," Kelly said. "And they'll spend the bucks to get a ranked program. Now you know who to sell on getting your team sponsored."

One of the first things Fowler had learned about Coleman Academy is that football ruled, webbing its arteries and veins into the hearts and the minds of trustees, booster parents, administrators, coaches, and students alike. Any attempt at new direction, as in this new bike team, only threatened the consuming passion.

"Football's their drug," Burkhart said. "That's because all they can do is sit their bulging booster b-rains on their bulging bleacher whoopee cushions. And something else I got to tell you right here about that football team." Skulking, snapping his teeth shut, he sat farther up and wrestled a banana out of his jersey pocket. "Look, Harper says I'm not a real man. He says it takes absolutely no coordination to pedal a bicycle—except he doesn't exactly say it that way, if you know what I mean. They're all like that. They come after me like I'm the last bite of meat on the c-arcass."

"They don't mess with me," Huffman said.

"Go wipe your beagle b-oogers on somebody else's—"

"Hey, hey!" Kelly grabbed at Burkhart's hand before he could throw his banana into Huffman's front spokes.

"You left your brain in your mother's womb. But you know that, H-uffman."

"You're getting mean." Kelly snapped two fingers in front of Burkhart's eyes to keep him from looking away.

"Look, we're supposed to go around all day yelling, 'Kick ass, Blodget! Kick some ass, Harper!' And what do those Neanderthal freaks do for you?" Burkhart's eyes iced. "They tell you that you shave your l-egs."

Huffman looked back and forth at Burkhart and Kelly. "So how about we put fart-licks—"

"Don't even milk it, Huffman," Kelly growled through closed teeth, raising a threatening finger from his right brake lever.

Burkhart punched at his computer display for maximum speed. "I've got it—TAMARACK." He stood up and stretched his legs. "I'll tell you one thing for sure. Nobody else's going to come up with a name like that."

"So TAMARACK—don't sound like a bicycle racing team," Huffman said. "You got us driving bulldozers. So you got us hammering subdivisions for the fattest couch wabingas in America if we go and start calling ourselves something like that."

"Blazing beagles! Huffman just said something half-way human."

"You don't call me a beag—"

"Shut up, H-uffman, because I've got the new name. TEAM HAMMERHEAD—no, just HAMMERHEAD. Bike racers do hammer, the last time I checked." Gesturing to the center of his white jersey where Kelly had shot him with red Gatorade, he said, "and look, it's perfect. A toothy shark and HAMMERHEAD, right here across our hearts."

"I still like fart-licks," Huffman said.

"On the sleeves," Fowler said, stitching his vision onto the new jersey, "we can put another shark, arching at the middle, and HAMMERHEAD BICYCLE RACING TEAM in a strong circle underneath it. A circle's one of the symbols of perfect and lasting movement."

Like Burkhart could ever listen to Fowler, but he went out of his way to look bored, to make Fowler feel invisible, to erase him from the team.

"Blue and lots of orange on this shirt. Eye-burning orange," he said.

"Jess and Brie have been good to this team," Kelly said.

"Get Pennington's somewhere—no, more sharks attacking this big school of wussy fish. Put all that right under the team name on the front and across the pockets on the back. Then, POWERED BY PENNINGTON'S slanted in some kind of real jazzy letters on top of a picture of Pennington's shop van ripping along behind the sharks."

Fowler pinched at the cleft in his chin. "I can see everything on this j-e-r-s-e-y so far. But something's off balance. We've got to get something up above the team name. Something on the top to coordinate all that other stuff down below."

"And here's something else," Burkhart said.

Something else. Burkhart talked like Fowler

hadn't said a word. But he filled up the top of the jersey, all right.

"Now here comes the hot sauce," he said. "Lots of white stars shooting out of the big shark and team name and bursting open up here across the top of the shoulders, front and back—just like the crest of a wave—so everybody has to keep looking at them. I'm talking power here. I'm talking fish or be fished. Hey, and as of two—no, one and one-half seconds ago, that's our creed. That goes on the shirt, too."

"I'm not riding another inch till I get that shirt," Huffman said.

"Not just shirts. I'm talking shorts, helmet and bike decals, gloves, water bottles, and socks. You've got to intimidate people. Psych them down. I want them grinding their teeth and drooling in their nightmares, 'HAMMERHEAD! It was a HAMMERHEAD!'"

"We've got to get that shirt, Coach. It'll make us ride faster," Huffman mewled in a little boy's manipulating voice.

"Yepper." Kelly zipped both hands into the

white and blue fabric above his head. "Pennington wants to buy into it, too, and Ro and I can pay off the rest of the set-up charges for you. If you three lumps of indigestion can ever decide what you want on it, we've got a new local company that could get us at least into that jersey by Fernandina. And I wanted to talk more to you about that, too."

Research informed the leaders of a small charitable organization that Jacksonville area bike riders liked to participate in fundraising tours. Interested in the possibility that they could increase their own budget for neglected children, they contacted Kelly to see if the new bike team at Coleman Academy would support a tour to Fernandina. Fowler couldn't wait. They would get to cross this huge river on the Mayport Ferry coming back into Jacksonville.

But Burkhart wasn't sold on this new program. MacLaughlin had infuriated him, refusing so far to authorize money for food in the event that organizers couldn't promise lunch, refusing even to sign his pledge sheet.

Unwilling to hear what Kelly was going to say about the ride, Burkhart cut him off. "Is the Mac Attack paying for our l-unches?"

"That's the only bad news."

Burkhart grabbed Kelly's arm. "Heil Headmaster can't buy us five measly lunches!" he blared.

He twisted his lips into a bitter sneer. "Hey, and I'm serious—that's priorities. That's just exactly how you HAMMERHEADS stack up in Big Macland. Besides the fact he never wanted a b-ike team in the first place."

"Cool down there, my little turbo tongue. It's not going to do us any—"

Kelly took the first blow.

No one was keeping an eye on the Volkswagen Beetle creeping along behind the bikes. A tattoo-shouldered man leaned out of the window on the passenger's side of the car and drove a baseball bat into Kelly's rear wheel.

Having failed to explode Kelly's tire, the shirtless man squeezed himself farther out of the window and took his second shot at Fowler.

But he missed his wheel.

Fowler made only a low, inner rumbling sound like distant thunder when the aluminum bat rocketed off his saddle and cut into his back.

"You lousy—sick!" Kelly shrieked, bursting into an angry pursuit of the blue VW Bug, accelerating now ahead of the riders.

"What's going on here!" Huffman broke for Kelly's draft. He grimaced at the hulking figure struggling himself back into the car.

"Get their license number! They just blasted Fowler with that baseball bat! But stay behind them! Stay back! They're sick!"

FIFTEEN

Two weeks had passed like stars and clouds. Fowler had recovered from the black and purple home run Bundy-Bat rifled into his spine, a local printer had rushed the order of the new team jerseys right onto everyone's backs, and the weather felt dry and sunny—what could've been a perfect day for a charity spin and ferryboat ride. But Huffman kept blowing "o" rings.

"I might have to stop again," he warned Kelly and sunk into the rear of the paceline behind Fowler.

"Let's see," Fowler calculated with overstated pleasure. "This makes the third stop, at an average of—let's say an average of ten to fifteen minutes. A few more stops, maybe. At this pace, we get to Fernandina around noon."

"That's only because you didn't spend the night

at Burkhart's," Huffman fired back, threatening Fowler with a bony fist.

He pulled himself up beside Burkhart and reached for his handlebar. Burkhart shot him an elbow.

"So Coach, he says they don't have steaks in Burkhartland, so I have to stuff myself with these roachy-looking beans and other garbage he keeps shoveling at me. Steamed carrots and apples. Junk like broccoli, or something that looked like broccoli tops. I don't know—he poured mashed yams all over them."

Huffman flicked his middle finger over his thigh at Burkhart, then kept shouting ahead at Kelly. "So I'm still starving before bed. He hits me with more of this papaya-apple-passion-pulpy-ginseng tea he made for dinner. Actually, that was pretty good stuff, so let me tell you about breakfast. Here he comes with these sunflower seeds, wheat berries, almonds, dates, raisins, and raw oats in yogurt he'd cut with water. So I'm reaching for the disposal switch, and he's spooning on peanut butter—oh man, and some little yellow doo-doos floating on top."

Still riding to the left of the paceline, he bolted forward and tapped at Kelly's arm. "No sugar." He grimaced around his nose and lips to show his disgust. "Burkhart's never heard of sugar. Says sugar's poison, and starts squeezing all this orange juice into a bowl. So that's ok, but he puts more yams in there, tosses it all in a blender, and tells me I have to drink three glasses. I'm sorry, I can't live like that." He huffed, shaking his head and tightening his brake levers to stop his bike.

The three other riders circled back to where Huffman was already stomping through high weeds on a hill falling off the side of the road.

"You ever notice something, H-uffman," Burkhart shouted at him, just as Huffman's brilliant new orange and blue team jersey disappeared into a heavy thicket beyond the weeds. "Hey, twenty-seven—no, thirty-two and a half years from this minute—scientists might g-et around to implanting you with the intelligence gene."

A cattle egret stretched himself into the air, hanging his white sheets out over the invisible lines of his territory.

"At least the fountain of youth picked a better spot this time," Fowler said. He watched the bird evaporate into the ghostly roughage of a deserted corn field. "Coach, no one bothered to tell you this, but Huffman dropped that last boom-boom surprise right in the middle of somebody's concrete patio. That was one serious moon landing, too." He chortled out loud and shook his head.

"So, when do we get to try this new and remarkable drainage system of yours?" Kelly asked Burkhart, breaking open his jar of repressed laughter.

"Go ahead—laugh your guts out. Just make sure they're full of—"

Burkhart pointed a crooked finger back at Kelly. "Hey, you tell me the difference between a chemical plant and a cereal box," he said. "Buy train-car loads of preservative—hey, s-oak the freaking stuff in n-itrosamines, sulfites, package it in dioxinized paper. And while they're at it, why is no one stopping them? I'm telling you something. A lot of good it'll do."

He picked at his front tire, then turned his cold blue eyes on Kelly. "You can read the greedy-ents. They're not interested in human life. They're interested in s-helf life."

A long and shrill yelp burst from the woods, stunning even Burkhart for a moment. "Maybe we got lucky, and he stepped on a pygmy rattler."

Huffman came struggling himself out of the thicket and back into the yawning weeds beside the road. "I was trying to pull my pants up," he said. "I backed into some stupid Spanish bayonet."

"You're lying through your teeth, too." Burkhart folded his arms across his chest, daring someone to speak—to defy him. "Those things don't grow wild."

"You think you're so right about everything all the time, so you go and back your—"

"Hey Hoss," Kelly said. He sucked at his cheeks to keep himself from laughing. "About that patio. I had no idea. Let's keep it in the woods from now on. The bayonets won't be quite so shocked as your new friends back down the road."

Burkhart took a few strokes at his cranks and then glided ahead of everyone else. "I'm glad it's not spring," he called back over his shoulder. "I'm telling you. We'd be stopping every t-en minutes to pick up the animals the freaking cars murder all over the—hey, some are still warm, one eye bobbing two inches at the end of their b-rains."

The wind splashed like waves through the high branches of the trees, sweeping in violent currents downward across the road. Fowler locked his cleats and pulled into the reorganizing line behind Kelly, his memory rushing with the bones and the fur—the raccoons, foxes, squirrels, birds—the frogs, armadillos, turtles—all the grounded blood purses he'd seen split open and left to rot.

"Tell Coach about that cow we found last year," Huffman shouted from the rear.

"Hey, I'm telling you." Burkhart fumed through his nose and lips and shook his fist into the air. "He was dead on the side of the road, and no one cared. We tried to pull him by his f-eet, but we couldn't move him. This dispatcher freak when I called the Sheriff, he got all over toasted with me—hey, you've got to hear this. He said he'd have it looked into. Like he was going to look into my—"

Burkhart wrenched a Clif Bar out of his jersey pocket. "We rode back out there. We went back the next day, too. Hey, I'm fifteen. Try to remind me how many more years I've got to live before they move that cow."

"We've got a truck rolling down on us back here," Huffman blared, cutting Burkhart off with a nervous clapping on his thigh. "Looks like a moving van, some kind of oversize truck."

"Pick up the pace!" Kelly shouted up and down the line. "Don't let him go by too fast!"

Huffman flattened his back over the top of his bike. "I hate it when those things pass me. The wheels come clear up to my handlebars."

Burkhart looked over his shoulder at the swelling leviathan creeping up behind him. "I'm telling you something. This is the last day I have to look at your ugly beagle face, H-uffman," he kept blaring. "You're sliding under that freaking truck. Your legs are snapping and bleeding. Your ribs, they're cutting into your—"

"Stick a sock in it, will ya!" Kelly threatened.

Fowler wrinkled the skin above his eyes, trying not to look at the black wheels quaking at his side. The truck rumbled past him, past Kelly, past Burkhart, and then pulled back into the right lane. He watched the creature shake itself around a bend in the road.

"So it's getting rough out here." Huffman gulped, his voice urgent—shrill and impatient like a frightened little boy who wants to butt into the conversation. "You never know who's coming up behind you anymore."

Like that drunk who slammed the man and his little girl on the Fuller-Warren Bridge, Fowler thought. It was on the news the week he moved to Jacksonville. The little girl burned to death.

Construction workers had traffic stopped on the

bridge. One of the workers estimated the DUI guy was hitting ninety to a hundred when he plowed into the back of the van. Suffering only minor bruises from the air bag that saved his life, the psycho swore he didn't see any flashing warning signs or any brake lights or any white delivery van stopped in front of him.

The girl's father couldn't help her. He was already dead and burning on his steering wheel. But that four-year-old girl. She was still alive, still trapped and shrieking against the back doors of the burning van.

Some man with arms Atlas would've envied tried to pry the doors open, but he couldn't bend the steel more than a few inches, and the van didn't have any windows back there he could break. This woman on the news said she had to stand there and listen to that little girl burn to death. The woman held her face and cried and said that was the worst noise she ever heard in her life—the hiss, the popping of her skin, her little eyes. She heard it, all right. She heard it with her stomach.

Of course, till somebody gets trapped and burned alive like that, the police and judges won't put the psychos in jail. That drunk got busted six times for DUI before he killed the little girl.

Fowler whistled a few times over his teeth to let the pressure out of his chest, then struggled to talk. "We've got people still driving out here after getting clipped twenty to thirty times for DUI. It was on the news."

"So my dad met one," Huffman said. "He's trying to run one night after dinner. Here comes this pick-up truck ripping a curve—the thing's on two wheels."

He pulled out of the paceline and rode up beside Kelly. "Burns to a stop. Just sits there cussing how he's going to toss my dad's wabinga over this wall that runs along the road." Huffman sniggered through his nose. "He's so doo-doo faced—can't tell you if he's in Florida or The Emerald City. So now he hurls his beer can, but the fairy's got his window rolled up, so beer's splashing all ov—"

He shook his middle finger at two car drivers

that honked and flew past him. "So it's not safe to run at night. So my dad's running down Greenland one morning about six-thirty before he eats breakfast. Here come these two garbage trucks. They're racing each other side-by-side. Hitting seventy, coming right at him on that part with the drainage ditch, or slime pond—whatever you want me to call the thing."

Another car honked behind Huffman. He motioned to Fowler that he wanted back into the paceline in front of him. "So they see him. One does the edge-over-closer-to-the-side-of-the-road-trick. My dad jumps onto this little bank above the ditch, but he loses his balance. Goes face-first right into all that slimy green—"

The car passed, and Huffman pulled himself back up beside Kelly. "So my mom says he can't come in the house reeking like that. Makes him undress in the garage. He's standing there all naked, and she's making him put his clothes right in the garbage can. So he wants to put something else in those cans, too. A little surprise for the garbage men."

"Right there it is. You ain't got no red, white, and blue neck," Burkhart said. "For one thing, Bubba don't see no motor on this here bike. Bubba don't see no ball neither. What Bubba does see is that lycra taillight of yours flashing out there in the breeze. What he does see is you've been shaving on those legs. Hey, Bubba got to k-ill you."

Nerves jumped in Fowler's back, crinkled along the soft tissue in his waist into a cold spot at the center of his spine. Bubba's got the tricks, all right, he thought.

Struggling after the move to find some piece of Jacksonville that felt like a real home, still lost in the memory, the worship of his childhood hills back in Pittsburgh, Fowler was searching one afternoon for the concrete hammocks Brie Pennington had told him about in Penny Farms. But one of America's finest good ole boys, unwilling to suffer the image of a man or a young man riding that bicycle down Thunder Road, infuriated by the lycra symbols alien to his motor-ball mentality, drove the outside mirror of his pick-up truck within a few inches of Fowler's arm, let go of the steering wheel, slid clear across the seat to the open passenger-side window, and spit a mouth-full of tobacco juice on him.

At first, Fowler thought Bubba spit coffee, but the brown liquid felt warm, not hot enough for coffee, and he could smell the tobacco. He could feel the warm muck clinging to his arm, clinging to his neck, to his ear, to his face near his eye, near his mouth.

"Dr. Burkhart doesn't like you, Coach," Huffman said. He tried to pull a Clif Bar out of Kelly's jersey pocket but kept sniggering, "you should hear what he says about you. He doesn't think you're a real man."

Only a cattle prod could've demanded more attention. Been less kind. Fowler squirmed in his saddle. In one of their private talks, Kelly had told him a secret. How he got roped into this reception at the beginning of the school year for the benefactors of the football complex expansion project, never

mind the fact Kelly would take one blue-light
special on a prostate test over all the parties in the
world. But he was doing fine. Three eight-hundred
dollar suits had him talking about the mountain
stages of the Tour de France when this red-eyed,
pink-faced batter-up for a heart attack came around
taking inventory—asking what everyone did for a
living. It was like Moses parting the waters right
there in his vodka glass when he hit on Kelly's three
big boys. But when he asked Kelly what he did,
when Kelly told him he was the tenth-grade English
teacher, the psycho just blinked on him, like he
wasn't looking at a real man, a real person, like
Kelly wasn't even standing there anymore. He had
erased him—blood-suckered himself right back
onto that investment banker, that portfolio manager,
that brain surgeon. And Fowler thought he was the
only one who burned garbage in his stomach.

"He doesn't want me hanging around no damn
teachers," Burkhart said. "He thinks they're all
flunkies who couldn't do anything else for a living,
so they watch TV all night and sit around all

summer. But you're his real pound key. I call you P-apa Kelly."

Huffman dodged pieces of broken glass littering the street in front of him. "So about this deal next Sunday." He looked at Burkhart and then at Kelly, dread rinsing the color out of his face. Kelly had been talking about a decent-sized criterium he wanted the boys to race in downtown Jacksonville the following Sunday. Fowler couldn't wait. He'd get to try more than club racing for the first time. But Huffman couldn't stop whining about it.

"So I mean, it's not safe spending the night with Burkhart," Huffman said. "Some fairy had to go and tell him how you can't get enough protein out of a spaghetti dinner. So what does he fix you? A tuna fish milk shake."

Huffman couldn't keep his eyes in his head. "So you think I'm kidding? He whips up this yogurt snot he makes with some kind of green oil. Then, while you're dialing 911, he's over there tossing in the macaroni shells, two cans of tuna fish, and pumpkin scrapings. You heard right, raw pumpkin innards.

Hands it to you in a glass, with a spoon. You get a spinach cookie for desert."

"Just because you have an eating disorder doesn't mean—hey, I'm going to tell you something. I'll tell you something right here." Burkhart mortared his anger with the rising pitch in his voice. "You can eat spaghetti for b-reakfast. You can carry it in your s-hirt instead of bananas. Hey, we'll toss on four—no, sixty-two meat balls. Freaking grease balls, H-uffman. No, hey, we've got to keep you huffing and puffing for that p-ink face and a heart attack. Triple by-pass—"

Burkhart shot his mouth full of Gatorade. "Hey, and I'm serious. I've been experimenting with these raisin, wheat germ, vanilla bean, and peanut muffins. No refined sugar, no salt, and I use extra virgin olive oil and my own applesauce to condition the dough," he said, his eyes Icelandic blue. "No hydrogenated—no bad oils. I got the kitchen smelling like the Muffin Nationals at Betty Crocker heaven, I pull those steaming breakfast cakes out of the oven, I break one apart and sprinkle it with one-hundred percent pure maple syrup—hey, I got to guarantee you something right here. You light yourself up with three or four of those pho-doggies, you're so full—"

"You're full of it. You're full of—"

A jackhammer shot off behind them.

Kelly shouted, "motorcycle!" and flattened his back more over the top of his bike.

Maybe the hulking figure was just sweeping to the right of the road, trying to find a smoother belt of pavement. Maybe he was insensitive, deaf to the violence of his tool. But Fowler had it figured this way. Just another bully.

"Get off! He's coming right at me!" Huffman roared at Fowler—trapped in his motion—bolted into the paceline beside him.

Their handlebars touched. They locked. Their wheels collapsed, and Huffman's right leg and shoulder slid across the meat-grinding road under his bike.

Huffman shrieked—screeched in raw agony—the asphalt ripping, chewing his skin and clothing eight to ten more feet before he slid and rolled to a stop.

He lay motionless, the road darkening under his back.

He squirmed. "You get back here, you–" he screeched again. "Look at my—look what he did to my shirt."

Fowler pulled at his own bike lying in the weeds along the surface of the road, but dropped it and ran ahead to Huffman, still cussing—still foaming and squirming—still finding holes and runs in his new team jersey—and blood on his leg, shoulder, and back.

"Don't touch me!" he shrieked when Fowler tugged at his wrist. Fowler could tell by the sting in Huffman's voice—by the sting in his eyes—that he was blaming him.

Kelly cranked back to where Huffman lay sprawling and moaning to himself. Guilt pulled his lower lip inside his teeth. "Can you move everything? Did you hit your head?"

"Look what he did to my shirt." Huffman

snarled around his lips, pulling at his sleeve to see the holes torn through the shark on his right arm and straining his neck to look at a long series of rips and runs down the upper part of his back. "Come back and try that again!"

"We're going to have to get you some new handlebar tape—maybe a new lever hood over here," Fowler babbled, not knowing what to say or to do, but tormented by the impotent feeling that he had to make up for some error—for some move, or lack of some move—that had contributed to Huffman's crash.

"Let's pull off at the first restaurant we find up ahead and wash that leg and shoulder," Kelly said. His fingers trembled at his side. "Maybe they have some Polysporin, or something. I want to look at that back, too."

"One thing's decided. I'm finding out where he lives."

SIXTEEN

A few people complained about the smell of pollution in the air. They stood in front of their team vans, arguing that whatever those chemical, coffee, and paper factories were cooking out there, the combined odor made the River Park area of the city smell like a toilet. Or something worse. A tall, gray-bearded man lectured at great length why the foul vapors stung the tissues inside his nose on windy, cool, and overcast mornings like this one.

More people drove toward empty parking spaces that bordered the St. Johns River—some in cars or trucks, some in vans or sport utility vehicles. Still others cranked on their tight-framed bicycles along Bay Street, or down the narrow park drive that twisted its way into a corporate plaza behind crowded registration and race-number pick-up tables.

First loud and synthesized music and then repeated instructions boomed from two large speaker cabinets, squatting like thick chimneys on the roof of a camper parked in the grass near the start and finish line.

Everyone please confirm or pay registration fees and then get out and try the course as soon as possible, a grainy voice kept blaring. Confirm your registration or sign on as quickly as you can. The first event of the race takes off right at eight.

Fowler pulled his registration form out of his team jersey pocket. He studied the mile and a half race course. He wondered how many other people thought it looked like a boot.

Whoever engineered the circuit took advantage of wide, multi-lane roads and a wide-open sweeping turn coming out of Oakmont Park Avenue onto Bay Street in order to maximize the possibilities of violent breakaways and sprints.

The faces even of the most experienced riders

discolored as they stared at the high road curbs, swelling like walls, wrapping themselves around the course. And the wind kept picking up speed by the hour.

"Have you tried it yet?" Huffman shouted. His eyes raced, rolling as if unattached, as he and Burkhart streamed toward Fowler. "So what's it like?"

Fowler released his grip on a small tree and pushed his bike into the narrow drive that squirmed its way through the river park. "Come on," he said, noticing that Burkhart had winced at the invitation in his voice. "I'll take you through it."

A few other riders cranked through the intersection that served the triple purpose of starting point, right-angle turn after the longest straight run of the circuit, and finish line.

"So I'm dreaming—this wind's trying to rip me off my bike." Huffman dropped his head and gripped the lower position of his handlebars. "I'd make a good sail."

"It keeps getting stronger, too."

"Can't hear a word you're saying," Huffman barked, standing up and cranking ahead of Fowler. Wind was plowing into their backs at twenty-five miles an hour—thirty, even thirty-five a few times. Fowler had never felt wind like this before. And it kept getting worse. At this point on the race circuit, nothing could block it. He looked at the miles of open space out over the river.

They surged a bit coming out of the intersection at Bay and Bridge Streets but then glided through the next ninety-degree turn onto First Street.

The asphalt darkened, as if someone had opened an invisible drain and the cold, gray light of the morning was being sucked out of the world. A few drops of silver rolled off the sheet-metal sky.

By the time they hit the headwind at Speedway, Huffman was threatening to go home. Fowler had heard Florida riders, including Huffman, talk about climbing the wind. Having climbed the foothills and mountains surrounding Pittsburgh, he hadn't been able to piece that metaphor together. Not until today.

The wind was flattening them like endless steamrollers. Fowler gripped the top position on his handlebars and pushed himself back on his saddle, like the riders back up north had taught him on the climbs. Earlier on Bay Street, he had seen birds flying west against this wind, hovering like helicopters over the river, over the parking lot.

Burkhart squinted ahead, then looked back over his shoulder and shook his head. "Diving for dollars starts on this channel right here," he said. "Jockeying for position ahead of that next turn."

They cut left and burrowed along a narrow, slightly descending, slightly twisting avenue, lined on its western side with tall office buildings that sheltered them in long intervals from the crosswind. Islands of pampasgrass and pine trees fronted a lake that shivered between two of the opulent buildings.

They ripped down the hill, clicking bigger gears, and railed through the turn onto Bay Street. The high curbs swelled—beat toward them like waves—long, savage, and cold.

"So you know it's all coming unglued down here

with Tornado Torcoletti pounding at our backs," Huffman said. "So be sure to smile and wave when you hit the front page of VELO NEWS, bleeding somewhere under a pile of thirty bikes."

"What I do k-now is, you smell like rotten chicken noodle soup, like you always do. Besides the fact you ride like a n-oodle," Burkhart said and hammered ahead of Huffman.

"The adrenalin's boiling out my ears!"

"I don't care how much filthy stuff they dangle in front of me." Burkhart waved his hand at Huffman to cut the pace. "No one's turning me into no prime junkie. I ain't no pack rat neither, so here's the deal."

He grabbed Huffman by the torn sleeve of his jersey. "You break up tempo for me at the front. If things get too rough, find yourself a hole and suck the fastest wheels till you get another chance to attack. When you scent a real opening—"

He pulled at his water bottle and wiggled his eyebrows. "That's when I make my move. I counter off your attack, then you stay back. Ride like a blood clot—ride across the front like a five-thirty traffic jam so I can get out and stay ahead."

He looked at Fowler—more like he looked through him. It was the stupidest thing. Like Fowler didn't already know he wasn't part of Burkhart's so-called deal—more like a slave ship than a bike team.

"You getting any of this, H-uffman?" he said, still glaring at Fowler. "Or let me guess—hey, I didn't come down here to do no hokey-poky, you bacon-belching Halloween mask. When you see me jump, you f-reaking do what I tell you."

Huffman turned up his cheeks and lips and nibbled something under his breath about duct tape.

"You think you got a better plan, beagle b-rains?" Burkhart tried to squeeze Huffman's brake lever.

"Not unless I get a chance to loosen your front wheel before we line up."

SEVENTEEN

People leaned against trees and sat in the park grass. Others wandered around, simpering with desire at the forest of brilliant bikes—visual echoes by Litespeed and Landshark, Pinarello, Colnago. The dark, stumpy cabinets of the PA system belted out music from the movie ROCKY.

"I won't bother telling you what this nose-job air's doing to my n-ose hairs." Burkhart skulked at the gray sky, then pushed his bike onto one of the terrazzo walkways leading to a two-story building that looked like a huge glass ship, ready to sail off into the tossing river.

"So take a whiff of what's coming up over here." Huffman was pointing at a tall, dark-haired figure in a Torcoletti jersey, his arms swinging like he was cross-country skiing through the grass. Skiing right at them.

Crell jerked to a stop in front of the scowling boys, pressing his hands into his chest, distorting his mouth and his eyes and pretending to faint with admiration over their new team jerseys. Then, shoving Burkhart's front wheel out of his way, he swaggered on down the sidewalk. "Don't piss in the baby pool when you get your chance to play bike racer out there today!" he yelled back over his shoulder, his arrogance dripping like the Niagara.

"Hey, and I'm serious. That's funny, Crell." Burkhart's face steamed red with anger. "I'll guarantee you something right here. Hey, we'll be leaving our VCRs on pause till we catch you on the O-RIFICE NETWORK."

"He knows he can rent space in your head." Fowler twisted his fingers through the folds in his jersey. "You of all people should—know that trick."

We had to make some last-minute changes for juniors fifteen to eighteen, the grainy voice boomed over the PA. All fifteen to eighteen-year-old juniors race in one field. I repeat, all juniors race in one field. We've moved the start time of that event back to eight o'clock. We'll repeat this announcement in five minutes.

Huffman's eyes were bouncing like superballs off Fowler and Burkhart. "So what's this?"

"For those of us who bothered to listen, it's exactly what the man just said." Burkhart grinned into himself, reaching down to readjust the Velcro straps on one of his riding shoes. "We get to rub against more riders who know what they're doing."

"Yeah, but where's Kelly?"

They waited another five minutes and then pushed their bikes toward a row of make-shift bleachers standing at the edge of the park along Bay Street. Kelly and Roberto came waving and shouting from the crowded area around the race-number and registration tables.

"Did you hear that announcement?" Kelly called to the nodding boys. "You were still under the official number—even after combining fields. But our rep talked the Gainesville team out of racing with the seniors and got you up to twenty-one.

Great training opportunity, guys. You're hot off the line with the strongest seventeen and eighteen-year-old riders in the Southeast."

Huffman rooted his tongue between his front teeth. "So what about the plan?"

"So what about it, H-uffman!"

"So I can just see us trying that kind of stuff now with those G-men flying all over us, B-urkhart. If you want to go and play bionic kid in an Uzi shower, that's your business. But I'm not getting my shirt ripped open again."

He searched everyone's face for agreement. "They're animals. They'll climb up our backs and ride right over our heads."

"Try not to wet your p-ants." Burkhart glowered at Huffman until he chewed at his lips and squeezed himself between Fowler and Kelly.

"Listen up, guys—"

The PA voice blared, All junior riders fifteen to eighteen report to the starting line, and a tense murmur buzzed through the people, standing like dark hills against the sky.

"Work together now," Kelly said. He reached to hold Burkhart's bike.

The boys stretched their legs, then hurried across the park grass toward Bay Street, their faces bleaching, lengthening.

Three traffic lights gasped red over the start/finish line.

EIGHTEEN

"You know the rules," the grainy-voiced man of the PA bellowed to twenty-one riders facing him at the line. Fowler had pictured this guy with red hair. He had to have red hair to motor his words the way he did. Or albino hair.

But Fowler wrinkled his nose and the skin above his eyebrows. It was more like looking at his doctor back in Pittsburgh. He still couldn't match the voice, but that face—those worried eyes. Like he was examining a bone cutting through an arm or a leg.

"You know you can't remove your helmets," the green-eyed man said. "If you get lapped, you're disqualified. If you keep riding, we're going to pull you off. You know the course is exactly one and one half miles, and you go thirty minutes plus two laps. Thirty minutes plus two laps, boys. You've got five places, and we've got five cash primes for you. The first lap's a twenty-five dollar prime. We'll call out the other four a lap ahead when you come around. The total purse is two-hundred fifty dollars." He paused, scowling as if distracted by some of the bikes in front of him. "How many of you are riding sew-ups?"

One of the Gainesville riders with long legs and a blond ponytail shook hands with the boys on the front of the line. His face widened, it inflamed into a brilliant smile, and he looked over both shoulders, calling "Go for it, guys!" to everyone behind him.

A pale and gangly, stringy boy talked without end, more to himself than to another rider grinning at his side. Others showed poker faces, guarded and silent, unwilling to give up the secrets they had warehoused behind their masks. Two dark-haired boys dressed in red team jerseys glared at the other riders, glared not in frustration—not, in fact, in anticipation—but with the frightening idiom that they could enjoy hurting someone.

No one stirred or spoke when the grainy-voiced man finished pinching granite tires. "Riders ready!"

No one breathed when he exploded his starting pistol.

A jittery pack swelled, loosened, and swelled again into the first right-angle turn onto First Street and through the jig-jagging turns heading for Speedway.

Burkhart ramped a bigger gear and flattened himself more over the top of his bike. "I'm overlapping you back here, Huffman." He grumbled under his breath and turned his head, grimacing at another kid trying his third time to dive on his position behind Huffman and one of the red-jersey boys driving the tempo into the headwind on Speedway. "Slam on me one more time. Just one more—"

But he didn't have to deliver his threat—three new riders leaned into the front, the pack gluing shut like a stream of mercury behind them.

Despite the usual dodging and jockeying for position, the surges, attacks, chases, and the sprints for the primes that race officials staged to whip up the egos of the riders, the pack kept stitching itself back together for the first five laps.

But then Fowler saw some boys starting to make the fatal errors. One unseasoned rider tried to shoot to the left of the peloton already cutting its groove across the turn off Bay onto Bridge Street. As if trapped at a gated crossing, the cars of a grunting train buzzing in front of him—trampling any thought of invasion—he squeezed his brakes and inched toward the high curb. Six—ten seconds and the rest of the pack melted onto Bridge Street—an oh-well-look streaking pink and gray across his face.

More riders were suffering the weight now of the turns and the wind. Scenting weakness, team workhorses attacked the limping pace at the front—battling for position fifty meters ahead of the downhill turn onto Oakmont.

Blood rushed through Fowler's head. He clicked a bigger gear and dug harder into his pedals—fighting the elbows—fighting to stay upright.

A second volley of attacks heading for Bay Street drove the front of the pack into a testosterone frenzy.

Chaos fed the animal, and two Gainesville boys whaled on the frontrunners, forcing them to the short side of the road.

Their ponytail leader dived for the line into the turn onto Bay Street—his other G-Man held back—blockading the rolling snakes bunching up behind him.

The pack broke loose like a cupful of marbles tossed onto the strip.

Burkhart flew out of his saddle to the right, Huffman shot to the left, Fowler criss-crossing a few meters behind them.

Five bikes collapsed and sparked across the asphalt.

NINETEEN

Fowler had managed to fast-dance around the crash, but struggled now to hold onto the rear of the reforming pack. Whip-lashed through the blocky turns heading for Speedway—feeling too sick in his stomach—too heavy to fight his way into a more favorable position, even at the slower pace grinding toward Oakmont—he started burning out of energy. And hope. Another field sprint boiling out of the sweeping turn onto Bay Street left him staring at the bleak asphalt. Alone.

He cranked onto Bridge Street—cranked with spaghetti-noodle legs through the battery of right-angle turns, and back into the bulldozer headwind on Speedway. His bike wobbled—the air thickened in his lungs—his vision blurred—it split—he thought he saw a pole coming at him.

"Work with me!" A red-haired boy had his hand on Fowler's shoulder. "Keep that pack from lapping us!"

Bunny hopping somebody's front wheel had freed the boy of the crash on Bay Street. Like Fowler, he had jumped a seat on the reforming peloton but got forced to the rear. Then shelled off the back.

Fowler folded himself into the other rider's draft and forced himself to speak through broken syllables. "I blew up. I'm dizzy. You're going to—" He took a desperate breath and shouted, "You're going to have to pull me a while!"

The red-haired boy tried to break him off his wheel.

TWENTY

The three Gainesville boys soared in a tight draft past the grandstands at Bay Street. Roberto studied his watch. Hammering like that, they've got to have at least a ninety-second lead, he calculated. With three minutes and two laps to go, and an average gain of thirty to forty-five seconds per lap—no one's going to pull these boys back. He tapped his watch and nodded at Kelly, then strained his eyes westward.

Burkhart, Huffman, and the fourth G-man railed through the turn onto Bay Street, tucked into each other like three boys jamming on a tandem.

"They're oiled!" Roberto dived onto Kelly's back. The two men wrestled and laughed and fell into the park grass along the street. "Man, that's locomotion!" Roberto tooted. "Chugga chugga motion!"

The fourth G-man, who had blocked traffic for his team at the first successful break of the race, had jumped ahead of the peloton right when Burkhart and Huffman broke away and had caught them churning into the wind at Speedway. The three riders were flying now a half lap ahead of the reformed pack that was chasing them. They couldn't win the race. Nor could they expect much external praise, but one of them would come in fourth. Another would nail down the final place.

TWENTY-ONE

"Someone's in the road up there!" Fowler called to the red-haired boy writhing in fatigue in front of him. The other rider wobbled his bike, but didn't say anything.

A woman was hesitating at the right curb ahead of the bleachers at Bay Street. A few people shouted, they whistled, but she pushed her baby stroller forward.

"She's coming out!" Fowler blared and shot to the right.

The other boy dodged to the left. He was delirious—he was bonking—driving straight at the crowd lining the street. He tried to stop, but his front wheel clawed into the high curb, exploding him and his bike into the air.

"That's a bad one," Kelly said. He tugged at

Roberto to follow him across the strip. Three men were already running toward the motionless boy and a few people who were trying to untangle him from his bike. A few other spectators cried and moaned.

Blood darkened one of the boy's wrists and the skin torn open on his arm. He groped for his riding glasses—stuck like a child's joke to one of his ears and his bleeding chin—and stared up at a man with receding hair.

The man bent down closer to the boy's face. "Can you hear me? Can you move your arms?"

He wore a starched blue shirt, pressed gray slacks, and small, round glasses. Not having seen emergency vehicles or paramedics, not even a first-aid kit at the registration area earlier, Fowler wondered if the man was a doctor.

"Point for me to anything that hurts."

The boy struggled to raise his head, to look up at the thin-haired man, but sank with exhausted effort back toward the sidewalk.

"Can you move everything? Do you hurt

anywhere?"

A bell rang across the street, and a large and swelling crowd whooped and clapped their hands.

"Easy! Get him up easy!" the man in the blue shirt warned two course marshals trying to pull the boy up by his arms.

Fowler stretched forward and cupped his hands around the back of his head. The two marshals supported his shoulders as he bent upward.

"He's lucky he didn't break his collar bone—or a few fingers," one of the marshals whispered to the man with thin hair. He shot a few breaths of air over his teeth and pressed his hands into his chest. He looked back at the trembling boy. "Are your father and mother here?"

Another bell went off across the street. The red-haired youth shook his head.

TWENTY-TWO

Six more individuals squeezed themselves into the crowd that swelled along Bay Street. They squeezed and wrenched themselves into slots along the curb that gave them a view up the strip. These people were neither the friends nor the parents of bike racers, Fowler figured. These people had never seen a bike race before, but they leaned forward, bobbing up and down.

They came to see passion and to look for heroes. They wanted to see power and strength, energy and resilience. Endurance. They wanted to see courage, sweat that was not their own. They came to shake themselves out of the boredom of their long suburban Sunday lives. They came to see violence.

They buzzed and they squirmed and stretched their necks. They stood on their toes and waved their arms—some smiling—some whistling and hollering—some twisting their hats with their rushing hands.

One blink, and the Gainesville riders were attacking each other like three greyhounds stretched out and flaming down the center of the six-lane strip. Another blink, they were sprinting out of their saddles, sawing their handlebars—crushing their legs and their arms into their bikes. The ponytailed captain muscled himself into the lead—four inches—eight inches—scoring by a wheel. A third blink, and the wide, gray street looked desolate, as if time had swallowed the boys.

Please do not step off the curb. Please stay off the race course, the grainy voice bellowed over the PA to restless spectators wandering into the street in front of the bleachers. You don't want to get hit by one of these bikes. The winner of this event just went over the line at thirty-eight miles an hour. More riders will be coming up any minute. Please, everybody listen. Stay completely out of the street.

Music from THE CHARIOTS OF FIRE

thundered back into the wind.

"This next battle could scald my retinas,"
Roberto said, lacing his fingers across his forehead
and squinting up the strip.

Burkhart was breaking out ahead of the
Gainesville boy and Huffman.

"He jumped too soon!" Kelly slapped his legs
and swatted at Roberto and Fowler.

Huffman attacked Burkhart's rear wheel, the
G-Man sprinting to catch Huffman's draft.

Burkhart dodged to the left and to the right,
trying to burn the other riders off his tail.

The G-man burst out of his saddle—attacked the
extreme left side of the street—sprinting for the
finish line.

Huffman took a straight head-shot
forward—firing his thick legs into his bike.

Not Huffman! Burkhart thought—losing his
eyes—losing his pedals.

Not Huffman! Not Huffman! he
exhaled—pumping the volcano in his lungs for one
more breath of air—for one more inch of the world

ahead of the passion and the violence whirling at his side.

TWENTY-THREE

Wind blew pieces of tissue and notebook
paper like white doves into the center of
the courtyard, already clamoring with students.
Fowler headed for a brick wall at the outer edge of
the insanity. But he hesitated, squeezing one eye
shut and squinting back at Kelly's balcony and dark
room. In all the weeks he had known him, Kelly
hadn't missed a second of school. He came early to
his room each morning, and he started class early,
too. But it was already eight-thirty, and there was
no note on his door.

Fowler leaned his bike against his unclaimed
wall and then rubbed his legs through his gray
slacks, forcing circulation into the soreness still
niggling in his thighs.

When he looked back up, Burkhart and

Huffman were rounding the corner of the
administration building. They came riding down the
gray sidewalk that led to Brooks Hall, dinning in
each other's ears about the race.

"You sucked wheels the whole last lap,"
Burkhart said. "Tell me you don't ride like a girl."

"So you tell me something. You tell me why
they put my name in the newspaper instead of—"

"Don't you even talk to me. You couldn't
outsprint a c-ircus bear on a unicycle."

"So look at who's talking. We went head-to-
head the last fifty meters. I handed you your doo-
doo."

Burkhart didn't say anything. He opened his
mouth and tensed his lips, ready to pick a
fight—ready to slam Huffman with insults before
he could score any more digs about the race—but
broken—defeated by his humiliation—he squeezed
a groan into his fist.

He tightened his brakes, shot his left foot out of
his pedal, and stood over his bike beside Fowler. He
stared up at Kelly's dark room. "Where is he?"

Fowler stepped forward and then crossed into Burkhart's line of vision.

"I said, where's Kelly."

"If you're bothering to talk to me, he's not up there," Fowler said.

"What do you mean, he's not u-p there?"

"I mean, he's not up there."

Burkhart burned a frown at Fowler. "One more time—just give me one excuse to—"

"It's been dark like that all morning."

Huffman rolled his eyes and tossed his hands into the air. "So maybe he's late."

"He's never late," Fowler said.

"So maybe he ate something last night."

"But there's no note or anything up there."

"Shut up a minute." Burkhart turned and started wheeling his bike back toward the heavy glass doors of the administration building. "Ok, you can come now, B-eagle Boy," he called over his shoulder.

TWENTY-FOUR

T all plants and a deep mauve carpet gave the entry hall to the administration building the look of a clean, quietly designed hotel lobby. Big Mac was singing in the blue wallpapered office to the right of the entrance. Two women stood laughing at his open door.

"Pretty bikes," a voice called from another open office door to the left. "Is anyone helping you boys?"

Burkhart looked at the woman smiling in front of him. He glanced to his right at a shelf lined with recent football trophies, a few water-color scenes of ducks and cows framed under glass, and the tooled wood moldings on the walls. Then, he studied the glowing woman again. Fowler could tell that he was tanked with all the attention and reward given to the efforts of football stars at Coleman and not the recognition even of bike jerseys for his sport.

"Do you know where Mr. Kelly is?" Burkhart said. He was scratching at something in his hair.

"Isn't he in his room?" the woman said.

"No, it's been dark all morning."

"Wait here a minute." The woman crossed the hall to another office. Almost as if she hadn't left, she returned with the Dean of Faculty and Students, a flat-nosed and puffy-faced man who could've been mistaken for a stuffed teddy bear, had he not dressed in the wool of a charcoal-gray suit.

"You're looking for Mr. Kelly?" the man said. The corners of his mouth turned into a kind but repressed smile.

"We checked his room," Fowler blurted out, anticipating the possibility that the man wouldn't give them credit for knowing where to look for teachers before classes.

"Teachers call when they're sick, or if they've had a conflict that could make them late." The Dean tapped a three-digit code into the lobby phone and looked at the three boys standing behind their bikes in front of him. His gentle smile no longer warmed his lips, but he raised a finger and said, "I'm calling his department head. Maybe he's running an errand somewhere on campus."

"His room's dark," Fowler said.

TWENTY-FIVE

The three boys stared at each other in the red-tiled courtyard that centered the u-shaped wings of Brooks Hall. No one had found a message, or heard any explanation for Kelly's disappearance, and students in his first-period English class had already been instructed to go to the library. A buzzer sawed through the quiet air, and a few girls rushed along the balconies and across the lower accesses to their bright classrooms.

"We're going to get demerits." Huffman was looking through rolling eyes at a closed door marked BIOLOGY a few meters in front of him.

Burkhart kept glaring at the sky, trying to erase a cloud sailing like nightmare popcorn over Brooks Hall. But he sat down on the edge of a large wooden planter, took off his Bass Weejuns, and started digging into his backpack for his riding shoes.

"So what're you doing?" Huffman asked.

"So what does it l-ook like I'm doing?" Burkhart peeled a blue sock from his left foot.

"So it looks like you're putting your riding shoes back on."

Fowler collapsed onto a long-railed bench and began wrapping a Velcro strap around his left leg to keep his slacks from catching in his chainring.

"So I get it. We're cutting biology?"

"No," Burkhart snapped back, jumping off his planter and pulling Huffman by the collar of his shirt toward the breezy mouth of the courtyard. "We're finding Kelly."

TWENTY-SIX

From the empty street, Kelly's two-bedroom house protected itself from total view behind a row of tall, dense azalea bushes. This guarded impression was reinforced by three palm trees that lined the narrow driveway to the right.

As expected for a school day, since Kelly always rode his bike to work, an old but well-maintained Chevy S-10 sat in the carport. In the bed of the dark blue pick-up truck was evidence of a custom-made bike rack, manufactured according to Kelly's specifications by a patient welder.

Lizards scurried along the walls of the stone and cedar carport. Blue jays and male cardinals flew back and forth across the yard, some landing on the cedar beams that crossed from the carport over a red-brick entry court. A gray cat stretched his legs, arched his back, and then rubbed his muzzle against the inside of the window that faced the courtyard.

"Where did he go?" Burkhart fixed his eyes on the wild ferns waving in a slight breeze to the right of his feet.

More birds landed on the cross beams, and a squirrel stood on his back feet in the grass along the driveway.

The birds pressed their worried sirens against their beaks.

TWENTY-SEVEN

The administration hall was quiet when Burkhart led Huffman and Fowler back through the heavy glass doors and across the expensive carpet to the Dean's office.

"Oh, yes, we've been trying to find you," he said when he opened his door and saw the three boys asking with their eyes if he had heard anything. "Dr. MacLaughlin wants to see you right away."

Fowler turned and followed Burkhart and Huffman to the office where earlier MacLaughlin had been singing. He stared at the blue wallpaper. He stared at the blue bench and two cordovan wingback chairs. He felt his stomach in his shoes. The Dean stopped in silence behind him.

Motioning everyone to come in, MacLaughlin punched three numbers into his phone and asked for orange juice and a plate of blueberry Danish. His free hand raced across the top of his desk.

"Roberto Ruiz called about an hour ago," he said. "He wants to see you—during lunch." He rolled a silver pen in his fingers. "It's difficult for me to tell you this."

Fowler gripped the arms of his chair. He felt his blood beating cold into his neck, into his forehead, and he trembled around his lips. He tried to focus his eyes on a window behind MacLaughlin's desk. The window quaked and it swelled—it rattled from the sound of three low-flying jets, grinding in their tight formation over the roofs of the school.

MacLaughlin raised his voice to speak over the deafening noise of the jets. "It's difficult—" he stumbled, he shouted. "Mr. Kelly died this morning at Memorial Hospital. His head was crushed under the rear wheel of a bus."

TWENTY-EIGHT

By the lunch hour, some version of Kelly's death had spread like a burst of food coloring into a small glass of water to every person at Coleman Academy. Although MacLaughlin had dispatched a memorandum to his teachers, a message to be used in class and in other appropriate settings according to their professional discretion, both faculty and students forgot details of the crisis, or added new ones, as they talked to each other during lunch.

And they talked to each other, all right. Stories about Kelly had always been popular in private gatherings at Coleman. Now, no one talked about anything else, only this bizarre and sudden death of a man whom they had all expected to see today. But for all the missing information that raised unanswerable questions about Kelly's death, as well as the climate or opportunity for distortion that grew along with the hours of the day, the only reliable account of the accident came from Roberto.

The metro bus driver had sworn to police officers that he had passed Kelly before he started edging his bus toward the curb on the long curve heading south out of San Marco. Roberto figured either that he didn't realize how fast bikes can take that bend in the road or that he forgot he had another fifty feet of bus still rolling along behind him—like a cat that forgets he has four legs and a tail creeping along behind his eyes, creeping along behind his whiskers.

Kelly must have looked at the white and blue walls of the bus pinching him on that curve. That's the only explanation why he didn't see a water drain—the ravenous kind of concrete drain that pitches its tongue up into the street. Sand and leaves pulled his front wheel out from under him on the plunging surface of the drain. His bike sparked the asphalt. It lodged in the mouth of the death Hoover.

The rear wheel of the bus cut the sharpest angle on the curve. Kelly saw the tandem axle. He saw the tire spinning down on him. He squirmed. But the rubber tread bit into his legs—crushed his knees—crushed his hips—chewed the skin and muscles and bones open on his stomach and chest. Something on the under-belly of the bus hooked the frame of his bike—dragged him another hundred meters on his face.

Two persistent police officers struggled with the faded, almost obliterated emergency numbers under Kelly's helmet and managed to contact Roberto. He was pouring pancake batter into a skillet when his phone rang at seven-fifteen.

Ten minutes later, Roberto walked at Kelly's side as paramedics wheeled his remains in a gurney along the gray pavement toward their ambulance.

The two officers told Roberto that they had picked bike parts and pieces of Kelly off the road for twenty minutes. Clumps of his hair and scalp, pieces of flesh torn from his shoulders and his face, broken teeth, the broken white tip of his finger blazed a trail to where he slid to a crimson stop, still braided into his bike.

The officers couldn't charge the bus driver with vehicular homicide. They couldn't even get him for failure to yield the right of way. But Roberto said the pink-faced genius wouldn't leave it with that. He had to start touching nerves, telling the policemen that if they had any brains they'd outlaw bikes.

"You just don't get it," one of the officers scolded back, punching his fingers into the operator's chest to make sure he was listening. "You're the moron. You just slaughtered a man with that bus."

TWENTY-NINE

Fowler didn't move. He didn't breathe. He sat like a figure on a shrine, a cold mass of stone guarding the head of Kelly's grave.

He saw a runner stop and stare a few minutes in his direction. Hyper, looking like he could do ads for energy bars in RUNNER'S WORLD, the little man with busy fingers pried a set of headphones off his blue cap, turned the volume dial at the base of his FM receiver. Twice he waved and started walking toward Fowler, but twice he hesitated.

Figuring he was just nosey or bored from running the narrow roads that furrowed their way between a stone wall and the story-book oak trees, which hung their arms and heavy moss over the graves, Fowler continued to study a wild fern he had pressed between his hands.

"Are you all right?" Trevor Daniels said. At first, he startled Fowler. He had run out of Fowler's field of vision but had changed his mind and walked up on his blind side. His voice boomed like he was shouting through a closed door.

For the greater part of a minute, Fowler stared at the man's Atlanta Braves baseball cap, its visor pulled low over his thick eyebrows.

"You've been sitting here like this all week," Daniels said, prying at the silence, rummaging now through the chest of Fowler's sacred creed. "I thought it was time to start asking—what I'm trying to say is, I just wanted to see if everything's ok."

Fowler looked back up, squinting into the sunlight, but no words came through his lips.

"Your father?" Daniels asked, nodding at the name carved into Kelly's headstone.

"He was my teacher at Coleman. And my coach."

"How did he die?"

Fowler stared at the head of Kelly's grave. A

pearl dropped from one of his eyes. "He was crushed by a bus."

"You don't have to talk about this if you—"

"A bus cut the corner for that last stop in San Marco," Fowler said. "It kept edging toward him. He didn't—he couldn't see a water drain in front of him. One of those psycho things that sticks out into the street."

In his mind, Fowler drifted back to the only time he ever saw Boots cry. They were trying to climb over a log blocking a path in the woods behind his house, and Boots started telling him how his grandfather got blown in half in Vietnam. How a Bouncing Betty blew his hips and legs off. But that's not what made Boots cry. He said his grandfather lived to see his intestines and a few torn pieces of his stomach trailing out of him into the grass.

Not that the DOT set water drains out there like mines to kill people. But they booby-trapped the streets, all right. And no one was ever going to convince Fowler they didn't get Kelly trapped underneath that bus. Ignoring phone calls and letters, ignoring a small but undeniable petition from commuters, recreational riders, racers, bike club members, and shop owners, they insisted they had no agenda to replace the things with the new style of drains they had coded for some other parts of the city, drains cut into a v shape behind the curb, with no tongue, no clam shell, no slippery metal cover, no steel slots running in the same direction as the traffic—no booby-traps sticking out into the street.

As if bicycles were going to disappear like dinosaurs, they said they had too many other priorities—too many needs greater than any sacrifice of city money they could justify to a handful of bike riders using public roads designed for motor vehicle transportation.

Some man went airborne—broke his collar bone, broke half his lower jaw, and two of his fingers. But the death engineers still wouldn't listen. And now they were refusing to dig up that psycho thing that killed Kelly.

Fowler strained to lift his head. He felt his eyes twitch. "He slid under—under the rear wheel of the bus." Scarlet warnings marbled in his eyes, and he struggled to look away. "His best friend got there right after they cleaned—him up."

Despite the suffering, the fear that illuminated this young man from the first moments he had seen and spoken to him, Daniels had been too curious—too selfish. He sat down. His cheeks burned with guilt—a troubled sense of respect. "I'm sorry I made you say that," he said.

"I-I thought he'd always be here," Fowler whispered.

"When you have something, you don't appreciate it enough. Maybe you can't."

"He always said we've got to cherish each other—stick to each other forever." Fowler caught his lower lip. "I did. I cherished him."

"I like how you aren't careful about what you say. Most everyone I know is either a politician or an alcoholic. Well, both. They think they have to play the game all the time. Then, they get good and sick of themselves and start drinking a lot of vodka and whiskey for breakfast."

Fowler nodded but didn't say anything.

"You probably figured it out, but I'm in the old deepfreeze myself." Daniels tensed his dark eyebrows in frustration. "I'm trying to run away from all that myself right now," he said. "Don't misunderstand me, I love my job. I love to sell. It's all I've ever wanted from the time I was a junior in high school. I thought I'd get to do things for other people and still have all the money and power and success. It's just I can't keep track of myself right now."

He cleared his throat so many times he had to cough. "The money's great. I can't fight that," he said, still cutting his words on a dry throat. "But I feel so fakey sometimes. One time, I was sitting in my car, just sitting there feeling sleepy and bored, waiting for my appointment with a client. And I started kind of dividing. It felt like I was out of my body looking at myself. Looking at my own face. And then, it really got me scared. I saw myself walking in my blue three-piece suit across the parking lot in the direction of my client's store. But I was still sitting in my car. It was—well, it was like seeing myself in a dream, in a movie. But I sure wasn't dreaming. I sure wasn't watching a movie."

He darkened his face with doubt. "Going home's worse. And I hate weekends. At least when I'm working, I don't have time to think about what I'm doing to myself. When it gets quiet, and I'm all alone for a while, that's when I really can't stand it. That's when I can't distract or trick myself anymore. That's when I get weird pains, too. My colon aches, and I start thinking about things like cancer. So, I run a lot. No one can find out about me here, or my—secret. One time, I even tried a marathon. Right here, all by myself. The only thing is, I can't ever get far enough away. I live right across the street in those condos."

"Going home's nothing I ever get too thrilled about either," Fowler said. "It's not just that my parents hate each other's guts and drink and fight all the time."

They didn't even answer the phone or keep anything to eat in the dark opulence of their water-front villa. They gave Fowler lots of money—he could always haul something in on his bike. But Kelly knew it, the poverty in wealth. Being just another kind of orphan, invisible and unrestrained.

In the diminishing light of a gray December afternoon in Pittsburgh, he caught himself staring out of the kitchen window at snow clumping down into the trees, melting onto the driveway, melting into the grass.

His father was on the run for the week checking his restaurants in New Castle, and his mother hadn't bothered to get up all day.

He pulled the blue shade over the window, feeling the soundless death of the kitchen creeping up his back.

He turned on the stove and oven lights, the track lights over the counters, the double row of canister lights, and the lights in the ceiling fan. He looked at the divided image of his face trapped behind two glass panes of the empty china cabinet.

He made the oven timer beep. He sharpened all the knives. He turned the empty blender on and off. He struck a silver spoon into the cereal bowls lying dirty on the counters and in the sink.

He struck books of matches. He lit candles. He opened the refrigerator door to spill cold light onto the gray tile floor.

"You start feeling pretty lonely after fifteen years of that kind of selfishness." More like emotional violence, Fowler thought. Looking at the orange and green neon stripes clashing on Daniel's running shoes, he said, "now, if you want to feel like you're a million miles from work or home." He spread two fingers apart and pointed at his bike.

"I was going to say, that's some frisky looking gadget. But go ahead."

"I tried baseball, basketball, swimming, tennis—I tried all kinds of running. But nothing speaks to me—nothing gets me inside myself like this bike. It's my favorite place to be. I can feel the tension going out of my stomach—like wringing water out of a towel."

Speaking of the blades in his stomach, the blades in his intestines. And now Daniels forcing conversation out of him like this at a time when he wanted to plug himself into his bike, all right. Ride through a hole in this lousy city. This lousy world. And never look back.

"So, tell me about Coleman," Daniels said. "Word is, they have the best looking chics in Jacksonville over there."

"I wouldn't know anything about that. The last girl who bothered to talk to me lives back up in Pittsburgh. Everybody at Coleman thinks I'm a freak, clear down to my so-called bike team. I hated the place the minute I walked into my first class."

"My father uprooted me from all my life-long friends, and just like you said, nobody would talk to me at my new school. I mean, I'd sit right there beside them in class and lunch—me, mister ocean mouth of the South—but they looked right through me like I wasn't even there, like I was invisible. Except this one extra-large-sized jock strap. He shoved me out of the lunch line. Thing is, I'm a little shrimp, but my neighbor where I used to live had this gym in his basement and traded karate and judo and jujitsu lessons for tossing me all over his basement for five years. I grabbed that four-letter hero on his arm and belt and kicked his legs out from under him."

He wanted to demonstrate, but Fowler said he got the picture and asked him to stop tugging on his arm. He remembered what Daniels had said about watching himself in a dream. It was like he was watching Daniels now—distant and alone.

"What I'm trying to say is, I hear what you're going through with this new school. But give it some time. You're a big, handsome guy. Things will change for you."

Reaching for a clump of mangled dirt on top of Kelly's grave, Fowler whispered, "the only person who ever really cared about me is—down there." He touched one of the sharks and then spread his fingers into the stars at the top of his team jersey. "He risked his job for me once. His whole way of life. I knew he liked me and wanted me around. I felt safe with him. I never felt alone."

Daniels picked at his headphones hinging on his neck. "I've always been able to get people to talk to me—sometimes when I shouldn't," he said. "I guess that's why everybody says I've got the gift of gab. I guess that's why they call me a born salesman. But for what it's worth, I'm sorry I hurt you."

"I wanted to sit with him—be there for him. But they wouldn't let me in." Fowler tightened his eyes in disbelief and shivered under his chin. "I kept messing around outside and knocking on the door, but they told me I couldn't see him. They told me—one of his eyes was hanging out of his head on a muscle."

THIRTY

A week after Kelly's death, Torcoletti announced that he'd like to sponsor a memorial race, soliciting patronage for the creation of the annual event from local and regional riders, bike clubs, and racing teams. At first, a lot of people thought the idea was obscene. Could he be so insulting? Could he be so crude, so egotistical, that he'd take advantage of another man's crisis in order to irrigate his rotting business?

A few of the older riders in Jacksonville even warned Burkhart and Huffman that Torcoletti would use Kelly's death as a lever to recruit them.

That warning exceeded rumored possibility one late afternoon when Fowler and the two other boys found Torcoletti waving and standing over his bike in the stone archway at Brooks Hall. But the silver-haired Italian looked tired. Guarded but frightened. He tried to smile but said only that he had something important to tell them.

For twenty minutes, as they cranked their bikes along San Jose Boulevard and down Beauclerc Road and Scott Mill Access, all he mentioned was that Fowler could use a longer top tube. But when they glided out of the turn onto Old Mandarin Road, commanding neither context nor introduction, he told the three young riders that they should stay together as the HAMMERHEADS. A lot of people would start coming after them, telling them what to do, telling them what to think, he said. But they had made something different, something solid here. They had made a commitment, a commitment to each other, and to the memory and the love of Kelly.

For the next ten minutes, he was quiet again. But with no more warning than the first time, he confessed that Kelly's death had made him think. Maybe for the first time in his life. He had always felt that time was his best friend, and all he had to do was to pedal through all the turns and strips, and sooner or later he'd get where he needed to go. But he had reached—he had dug so hard for so many dreams. And where was his good friend time now?

He used to have a theory—a belief, he called it—that if you stuffed yourself too full of life every day, you would never fear death. It's like eating too much pasta. You can't eat any more. You can't even stand the sight or the smell of more food. You're sick of it. If you have to die, do it on a full stomach. Die when you're stuffed full of life.

But his stomach hadn't been very full lately, and Kelly's crisis had taught him something new about the world. One little mistake. One blink of the mind. No matter how good you are, no matter how much you know, no matter how alert and sharp you are, that's all it takes to get yourself smashed under a bus.

You can't keep making yourself believe that you're special—that horrible things happen to everyone else, not to you. Time might be your best friend, but it can also wash you away at a point when you're still too hungry to die—when you've got too many things left undone.

All those car drivers out there who hate bikes and what we do with them are probably right, he kept saying. We should just park these things and find some other sport like tennis. Some safe place. Some place guarded by a fence.

But it was only his lips that said it. He may not be the world-class rider that he had churned all his life to be, but this was what he was born to do, what his legs were meant to do. Tucking into his bike. Tucking into other racers, people who knew how to take him seriously. Tucking into himself. This was what spoke to Silvio Torcoletti. This was his own little hole in the wind.

Yes, he was being selfish with this race, but Fowler caught the paradox in Torcoletti's confessions. Kelly must not go down as the scapegoat. His death must not be the reason, the excuse why people put away their bikes in fear. Kelly's death must become not the ironic means to the end, not a more convenient way for politicians to deny the money to pave abandoned railroad beds and to network the city streets with lined shoulders and safe bike lanes, but the declaration, the protest, the moral ether reminding riders that their needs were true. And necessary.

At first, Torcoletti had planned a criterium, wanting the drama and the passion, and had even told a few people that he was thinking about the same course as the race two Sundays ago along the river in downtown Jacksonville. But in more direct tribute to Kelly, in order to draw effective attention to the relative safety of where Papa Kelly had encouraged his boys and his friends and countless other riders to train, he announced that he was sponsoring THE FIRST ANNUAL WOOD KELLY MEMORIAL ROAD RACE in Old Mandarin.

THIRTY-ONE

By ten after six, a few people were unloading
their bikes and stirring around a long,
warped-looking table that one of Torcoletti's friends
had placed at the intersection of County Road
Thirteen and Old Mandarin Road. The race would
end thirty miles north, one-quarter mile ahead of the
intersection of Scott Mill Access and Beauclerc
Road. This would give the racers a small hill to
climb and then a gutsy one-half mile straight run to
the finish line.

Two riders came from St. Augustine and a few
more had driven from Palatka, Palm Coast,
Daytona, and from Ormond Beach, thus increasing
the number of racers in each category, but by seven-
thirty, Torcoletti stood shaking his head, realizing
that fields were still too small for more than two

separate events.

He complained in Italian and then in English that people were afraid to do what they knew was right and decent. "Wha-suh madder yous. No money—nobody comes a race." He pawed in the grass with his shoe, and growled—cussed again in Italian.

Roberto straightened an arm and drummed on Torcoletti's shoulder. "You advertise no purse—you get no pack. You're fighting the American Dream, man."

Torcoletti nodded but dropped his head.

"But never doubt the blessing in disguise," Roberto said. "Mix all juniors into one field, and all seniors and masters into another. Not only does this give experienced riders an opportunity to fine-tune their road work, but everyone else gets a good chance to learn something new. You know Kelly would like that."

Torcoletti nodded. He called to everyone to be silent for five minutes, his voice stepping into the wind that rolled like waves through the trees above his silver head.

THIRTY-TWO

The older riders cleated into their pedals and hammered out of sight at eight o'clock. At eight-fifteen, a few juniors pushed their bikes out of the grass and started lumbering their way down the pavement toward the starting line. Two other boys dressed in red and green team jerseys were loading their trainers into a van.

Huffman had disappeared. Burkhart and Fowler stood over their bikes a few meters from the abandoned registration table. Fowler tried to ask how Burkhart wanted him to lead out the breaks, but he never said a word. He never bothered to look up either, busying his concentration instead on a banana he was eating, one thin nibble at a time. He didn't say anything until Huffman rolled back up beside him.

"Let me guess—hey, l-ook up here when I talk to you. You've been taking asphalt samples for me with that piece of bacon you call a tongue." He dropped his banana peel over Huffman's front tire.

Huffman shrugged his thick shoulders and pointed toward County Road Thirteen. "Headed up to the old quick sack, and I'm not talking cooler cases, if you get what I mean."

Burkhart shoved Huffman in the arm and then faced the long curve that made the race course disappear into the woods ahead of him. He shook a fist back at Fowler. "You're just in the way," he said, still not bothering to turn around. "Don't you ever forget that."

THIRTY-THREE

Fowler rolled his front wheel forward to the white chalk line that squirmed with nervous energy across the road. Other boys settled into their places to his right, to his left, some of them whispering, but nothing he could make out.

"Protect your handlebars when you bunch up in the turns," the start official said. A few boys grimaced and stretched over their bikes, a few others snapped their brake levers, but no one spoke now.

"Use your elbows. Use whatever it takes. I don't have a problem with that. But no slug-fest." The man turned eyes that could freeze a rock slide on two kids smirking at each other—screwing up their faces with sneers.

"No body shots, no handlebar shots. No hip

bumping. You know what I mean." He crossed the chalk line and pried himself between the two boys, straining their lips to suppress their embarrassment, their crude and violent disbelief.

"We have no cash prizes for you. No cash or bonus sprints. No purse. This is a memorial race, plain and simple. You're racing for the love, the dignity, the preservation of the sport. What used to be called honor and good sportsmanship, before the gods—"

The man walked into the grass at the side of the pavement. He was grumbling to himself, something about cheaters, but Fowler couldn't hear it all. "Before the gods of money and steroids, blood doping, win-at-all-cost—like I said, you know what I mean." He drilled those eyes back into the two kids.

He raised his hand into the air. Fowler squinted at the sun burning between two of his fingers.

He moved his lips, he dropped his hand, and the fifteen riders surged for the curve that bent the road into the trees.

One boy broke out on his own, diving for the mouth of the fast turn, but the pack swallowed him a hundred meters into the first straight run of the race.

Another boy tried to stiff-arm a tall, dark-haired eighteen-year-old in the shoulder but missed and hit him in the neck and lower jaw. Two riders cussed and ordered the hostile kid to get out of the race. He swung at the two other boys.

By the halfway point, the pack was cooking again, team workhorses and a few unattached riders pushing the pace and attacking each other at the front. The pack narrowed, swelled, and narrowed again into a long, thin column sucking leaves out of the side of the road. Sucking, rolling like a flash flood under the thickening canopy of oaks.

Four miles, five miles—and a few heads started to roll. Another two hundred meters, three hundred meters—more heads loosened, and the frontrunners slowed their pace, sinking under the weight of their crushing labor, the fire in their lungs and their legs.

Fowler's head spun around—it stormed with

thoughts of Kelly. Come on, man! Un-hitch that Winnebago! he could hear Kelly sounding the alarm at his back. He could feel him. He knew he was there.

He whirled himself into a sprint—breaking out of a sweeping curve into a three hundred meter stretch of road fed by a gusty tailwind—feeling his pulse ticking—feeling strong—his muscles jumping in his legs, in his arms—inspiring, demanding new fury—new and desperate vitality—rocketing his bike down the center of Old Mandarin Road.

The pack was blowing apart behind him, riders sprinting and dodging all over the road as if someone had dropped tormented rattlesnakes under their bikes.

"We're towing someone back here!" Huffman warned Burkhart, cutting to the right and to the left, when he and Burkhart caught Fowler's draft. "Two more—we got two more chasing us!"

The three boys surged and whipped in and out of the shadows flowing across the road—trying to spring the alien rider off their tail.

They criss-crossed—four, five violent bursts to opposite sides of the road—then shot back together to the left, Burkhart dodging back out to the right.

Hurting now—suffering from any chance to catch a draft—the other rider wiped at a rope of saliva trailing off his lips, trailing off his chin.

He wobbled his bike. He skated on his front wheel.

Burkhart jumped out in front of him, opening a gap. Fowler and Huffman sprinted to catch his line. The three boys tucked into each other and dived like rolling magnets through another curve in the road sweeping to the right.

THIRTY-FOUR

Fowler pulled Huffman and Burkhart past shaded lakes and creeks, past dark acres of rolling woods and empty-looking houses half concealed by pine and oak trees. At the crest of the final hill that brightened with the white, open glare of the morning sun, he whistled a few breaths over his teeth, repositioned himself to the left, and sailed onto the rear of the paceline. He studied Burkhart's tireless legs. He thought about the cold and measured strokes of a timing device, ticking down to zero.

With one-half mile to go, and with no other riders or teams driving a chase behind them, not that Fowler could see at least, Burkhart was bound to push on him—bound to put a wheel across his line—trash his handlebars—deal some trick to break him. To break Huffman.

"No one's back here yet!" Fowler shouted.

He had never motored this close to the front of a race, but Fowler had it figured this way. Burkhart was dangerous. Burkhart thought like an animal. Burkhart didn't think at all. All Burkhart cared about right now was evening the score—more like evening the shame—of the last race with Huffman.

That meant destroying Huffman. Ravaging the thick yet still unsettled dream that parceled his dominion—the dignity, the urging confidence that promised Beagle Boy real talent, real strike in his legs. Not just a one-time lucky sprint.

And that meant destroying Fowler.

He stared at the hammerheads attacking the other fish on the back of Burkhart's jersey. Nothing ever changed. Nothing ever did. Mad blood honked like an ancient code in that extra slab of meat that clamped Burkhart down instead of a human brain.

A small number of people jumped in the grass and stretched their arms into the road two hundred meters ahead at the finish line. The people clapped their hands and chewed their fingers.

Huffman fired his signature head-shot straight off the front of the paceline.

Burkhart broke off Fowler's wheel—rushing like white water for Huffman's back.

He was wild.

Up and hunting. Breathing adrenalin instead of air.

But he cut his rpm. The psycho had torqued himself out in front of Huffman, but he hovered over his bike.

"That f-reaking bus!" he roared at the puny crowd waving and springing up and down—coaxing him to come on and sprint for the line. "This is his race! His!"

Burkhart dropped into his saddle. He looked over his shoulder at Huffman and Fowler laboring to catch his rear wheel.

"We're Kelly's kids," he said. "Come on! We're Kelly's kids! Kelly's kids!" he blared a second and third time, reaching for Huffman's hand.

He straightened out his other arm and called

back to Fowler. "You getting any of this, Fowler?" he said, his eyes resting at the center of a bold, new axis.

Fowler took his hand—felt his grip, strong and certain—the herald of an imperishable truth—bright as the earth.

He hadn't drowned in the black river of doubt cutting scars, telling him that he couldn't count on anyone, that no one wanted him, not his mother, not his best friend. Fowler was Kelly's mind spring—his living witness now that patience is our sanity.

"Hey," Burkhart said. "You're going to have to start hanging out at my house like Bow-Wow Billy here."

Fowler tried to picture eating one of Burkhart's spinach cookies. And he'd been talking about this new icing he wanted to make in that looney blender of his. This fig paste stuff with yogurt, olive oil, honey, asparagus, and yams. Fowler smiled and bobbed his head at Burkhart and Huffman.

And they glided side-by-side over the chalk